IRON NEST

WAR FOR NEW TERRA ✪ BOOK 2

T.W.M. ASHFORD

Copyright © 2022 by T.W.M. Ashford
All rights reserved.

No part of this book may be reproduced in any form or by any electronic or mechanical means, including information storage and retrieval systems, without written permission from the author, except for the use of brief quotations in a book review.

Any characters in this publication are fictitious and any resemblance to real persons, living or dead, is purely coincidental.

Cover design by Tom Ashford

DARK STAR PANORAMA

The *Dark Star Panorama* is the shared universe of sci-fi stories in which *War for New Terra* takes place.

To hear about new releases and receive an exclusive, free prequel story set in the *Final Dawn* series, sign up for T.W.M. Ashford's mailing list at the website below.

www.twmashford.com

IRON NEST

CHAPTER ONE

The transporter truck rumbled along its weathered tracks, its thick fuselage muffling the sound of explosions outside. As far as anyone sitting inside was concerned, they may as well have been riding in a drop ship. But there were still too many bug cannons to risk an aerial approach.

"I would have thought we'd have mech suits by now, or summin," said Private Evans, wincing as another blast went off nearby. "You know? Or like, robots to do the fighting for us."

"The UEC has been constructing a fleet of Arks and battlecruisers since before we were born," Sergeant Rogers snapped. She shivered with her arms folded over her chest. "And for the past year they've spent every last cent humanity has laying the foundations for this planet's future cities. When do you think they had the time or resources to build you a robot army, idiot?"

"Go easy on him, Ginger." Ghost smirked in the seat beside her. "Evans hasn't done much more than guard a latrine since he got here."

"Come on, that ain't Evans's fault." Duke bumped Evans

with a shoulder the size of a beach ball. "Command chooses who goes where and does what, not us."

Ginger supposed Duke was right, as per usual. But that didn't mean Evans wasn't an utter cretin all the same. Yes, she wished that humanity wasn't still semi-dependent on diesel-guzzling tanks and firearm tech from the best part of a century ago. She wished that one of the thousands of more advanced alien races around the galaxy would give them a hand in clearing out New Terra's bug infestation, too. But they had to make do with the hand they were dealt. There was no sense in hoping for anything else.

"Just don't forget that if they didn't need us to fight, we wouldn't be here. We'd be back on Earth, dead like everyone else."

"All right, Sergeant Rogers, that's enough." Staff Sergeant Baker turned back from the partition separating the bulk of the transporter from the drivers' cabin up front. "No need to scare the new guy. I assigned Private Evans to Fireteam Sigma so you could shape him into being the best, not humiliate him."

"Can't do one without the other," Ginger replied. "Sir."

"Thirty seconds out," Baker shouted, ignoring her last comment. "Helmets on and safeties off, people. This is gonna be a rough one."

"When is it not?" grumbled a private further down, flexing his frozen fingers.

There were thirteen people inside the transporter – three fireteams containing four marines each, plus Staff Sergeant Baker. Not to forget the two drivers up front, of course. Those about to enter the fray were sat in two rows of six along the transporter's hull, facing inwards towards each other. Everyone hurriedly checked that their helmets were strapped on tight and they hadn't left their med kits and multitools back at base – checks that they all performed half a dozen times before even setting off.

Iron Nest was one operation *nobody* wanted to be a part of. Nerves were especially high.

Ginger flicked off the safety on her battle rifle but kept her fingers clear of the trigger. The transporter was bumping up and down over the rugged terrain, and the last thing anyone needed was a bullet to the head before they even opened the doors. Ghost had her sniper rifle resting against the seat between her legs but would sling it over her shoulder as soon as she got up. Until the situation called for it, she was better off with her submachine gun to hand.

The transporter lurched to a stop. Everybody clattered into one another along their benches and let out nauseous groans. For a second Ginger thought that was it – they'd arrived. But Baker gave no order, and moments later the transporter was moving again – first doing a violent, stomach-jostling about-turn manoeuvre and then reversing at great speed in the same direction they were originally headed. She could hear the belching engines of other transporters nearby doing the same.

That's when the chitin rounds started.

A wave of brittle bullets pinged down both sides of the transporter. Everybody riding inside flinched, including Ginger. But none of the organic projectiles made it through the vehicle's armour. Everything was reinforced. In the months following the somewhat disastrous initial invasion, Command had made sure of it.

"Jesus Christ," Evans groaned. "I thought Command took out the heavies already."

"Fifteen seconds," Baker shouted. He was standing in the centre of the fuselage with his hand pressed up against the roof just like when they flew in the drop ship together.

"Get it together, people. We knew this was coming. We were trained for this."

Trained for it? Ginger would have laughed if she hadn't been on the verge of throwing up in terror. To say they were trained was a bit of a stretch. Those in the transporter had simply survived long enough to know what they were dealing with.

"Ten seconds," Baker continued. "On your feet, marines. When those doors open, keep your heads down and push forward. And don't stop pushing forward, no matter what. Do you hear me?"

The twelve other marines, now standing clustered together in the centre of the transporter, gritted their teeth and barked out their reply as one.

"Yes, sir!"

Ginger tried to keep her breathing under control as the pinging of chitin rounds and the thunderous artillery grew even more regular. They'd been driving for over an hour already. She'd received a briefing, of course, same as everyone else. But that only did so much to prepare her for whatever lay waiting for them once they stopped.

The transporter shuddered to a halt. Somebody let out a nervous whine. Ginger tightened her gloved grip around the handguard of her rifle.

A second passed. It felt like forever.

The red light at the back of the transporter turned green. At the same time, a deafening alarm rang out. The doors at the rear of the truck automatically flew open.

"Go!" Baker screamed behind them.

Everybody crowded out through the narrow exit. No sooner did the first marine's boot hit the ramp than a fresh storm of chitin rounds came screaming their way. That first marine screeched as inch-long pieces of bony, shell-like projectiles tore through the gaps in his chest plate. He toppled off the side of the ramp, the front of his body a pulpy, bloody mess. His boot, severed at the ankle, stayed exactly where it was.

"Keep going!" Baker yelled, shoving the marines at the back. "Don't stop pushing forward!"

Ginger bowed her head so that barely any of her face showed; she saw Ghost, Duke and Evans do the same. Good. Nobody was going to die before at *least* setting foot on the ground. Not on her watch. Then they started pushing, too. If people panicked and tried to stay where they were, they'd all die. The transporter was quickly becoming what Ginger feared most: a bottleneck.

More troops were being cut down in the doorway – Ginger could see their black silhouettes shake and fall against the blinding white of the world outside. A brushstroke of blood swept across the inside wall of the truck beside her, but still she kept pushing.

Half of their survival would come down to keeping calm under pressure.

The other half? Luck.

Ginger was close to the transporter door herself, now. The chitin rounds continued to pepper the metal chassis of the truck with gut-wrenching *pings* and *donks*. She could hear explosions, too. Whether they were caused by humanity or the bugs, she had no clue. One marine remained ahead of her – between the marine and the glare from outside, there wasn't much of a view.

And yet *all* she could stare at was that harrowing, unknowable whiteness outside, and the instant death that lay within it. Blood pumped through her temples, tunnelling the periphery of her vision. She tried to swallow and found she couldn't.

This was it. This was the end.

A single chitin round caught the marine in front of Ginger in the neck, spurting claret down the ramp. In her dying panic, the soldier clutched at her throat and tried to rush back inside the transporter. Ginger couldn't allow this for two reasons. One, the resulting chaos would get her and the rest of Fireteam Sigma killed as well. And two, the inside of the vehicle wasn't much safer than the outside. At least if they pushed forward they might find cover and dope the poor woman up with morphine.

Ginger grabbed the straps of the marine's backpack and, ignoring the jets of blood gushing from her neck (and occasionally spraying droplets across Ginger's face, which she didn't notice until later), pushed the private further down the ramp. The marine – a Private Murphy, if Ginger's recollection served her well – protested, but her words came out in a garbled mess and, with one hand trying to stem the bleeding from her neck, she hadn't the strength to resist. Ginger felt a hand grab hold of her shoulder from behind and knew that Ghost was helping push, too.

"For the love of God, move!"

Staff Sergeant Baker's words were but a blurred memory happening someplace else. She was fighting with all the strength she had. It wasn't *her* fault the whole operation had gone to hell within seconds of it starting. And it really had been only seconds since the transporter doors first opened, even though time seemed to have adopted a warmer, more viscous quality since, trickling out through the door alongside the troops like hot tar from an open pipe.

She shoved Private Murphy even harder.

The plan was always to get her someplace safe, away from the assault. Maybe to even find a medic out there on the battlefield who could save her life. Ginger would swear to this until her dying day. But the incoming fire didn't cease for a moment, and seconds later a trio of shards rattled against Murphy's chest. The first shattered harmlessly against the marine's protective padding, but the next two sunk deep into her flesh. She screamed out in pain, and then the arm raised to her neck went limp.

Ginger kept hold of Private Murphy. She couldn't let her fall. There was no way of knowing for sure whether Murphy was dead, unconscious from the shock or simply paralysed, one of the chitin rounds having severed her spinal column. Either way, there was surely no saving her now. But that didn't mean Murphy couldn't still help save the lives of her fellow marines.

More rounds punctured Murphy's body as she pushed forward, Ghost's reassuring hand still gripping Ginger's shoulder tight. If poor Private Murphy wasn't dead before, she was now. One round even hit her face with a sickening crunch, rolling her helmet backwards. Ginger screamed outwardly while she apologised silently inside her head. But she didn't let go. Though Murphy had grown heavier, at least she wasn't resisting anymore, and moments later they reached the bottom of the ramp.

Ginger spotted a rock poking out from the tundra only half a dozen metres ahead of their position. She let Private Murphy's body topple to the ground and, together with Ghost, sprinted into cover behind it.

"Jesus Christ," Ghost moaned as she slammed herself against the rock. "That was pretty frickin' dark, Ginger."

"If I hadn't used her as a shield, all three of us would be dead now. Please don't make me feel any worse than I do already."

"I know, I know." Ghost winced as a stream of chitin rounds shattered across the white peak of the rock. "If I was dead and you were next, I'd want you to do it too. Just bleak, s'all."

Ginger grabbed a fistful of snow and mushed it against her forehead. She felt like she was on fire. Guilt, adrenaline, good old overheating – whatever the reason, the cold didn't do much to alleviate it, and her glove came back watery and red.

"I can't get used to all this snow." She wiped her glove on the ground. "It goes on forever."

"We got this stuff back in England, apparently," Ghost said, her chest heaving up and down as she gasped for air. "Until it got too hot, obviously."

"Right, breather's over." Ginger's words turned to steam as she pointed to the top of the rock. "Tell me what you see."

As Ghost clambered up, Ginger looked back down the line. Other fireteams were crowded behind similar rocks and metal barriers erected by an earlier scouting party. This stage of the operation involved hundreds of marines in total. God only knew how many of them were dead already.

Bodies were piled up in the snow, their blood staining the otherwise untouched tundra a dark red. As she sat there behind the rock, Ginger watched as torrent after torrent of chitin rounds sprayed past them, shattering against the rocks and transporters or cutting down the marines still trying to make their way into cover. Marines to her left and right winced and screamed, either in agony or frustration in not being able to push any further forward. A few tried firing their battle rifles back but couldn't get a proper look at the enemy. One soldier back at the transporters – a couple of which were nothing but smoking husks now – had lost one of his legs when the doors opened and was crying and moaning as he crawled desperately to safety, the snow too fine and too deep for him to get any real purchase.

"How does it look out there?" she asked Ghost, unable to bear watching the poor man suffer any longer.

Private Flores stood on a pair of stony ledges a couple of feet above Ginger's head. She'd laid her rifle across the flat top of the rock and was scrutinising the battlefield ahead through its scope.

"About as FUBAR as it seems back here," she replied. "Lots of open space with not much cover. Most of the bugs past the first trench are mutants rather than roaches. They're dug in pretty deep, and—"

Another wave of projectiles crashed against the rock. Ghost lost her footing and flailed backwards towards the ground. Luckily, the snow softened her fall. Her rifle clattered down the rock behind her.

"Sons of..." Ghost grabbed her weapon and tucked herself back into cover beside Ginger. "I guess they really don't want visitors, right?"

They both jumped as two loud booms momentarily drowned out the sound of screaming and rifle fire. Ginger raised her head and spotted an egg sac launch into the sky from somewhere further ahead.

"And that's why we couldn't fly in," she grumbled, watching the green inferno coast overhead. She could hear the rippling of the flames billowing out behind like a comet's tail.

The explosive sac came down much closer than Ginger anticipated. It plummeted onto one of the transporter trucks further down the line to their right, instantly reducing it to a smouldering heap of blackened steel. A second egg sac crashed into the ground beside another transporter, this time on the far left. The vehicle tried to pull away only for its fuel tank to ignite a moment later, blowing its sides off and roasting its drivers alive.

The remaining transporters – almost three dozen in total – rapidly accelerated back into the great white tundra to escape the cannons' range. Ginger swore. If Command later ordered a retreat, they'd be making the trip back on foot.

Sure enough, dozens more egg sacs were catapulted into the sky after them. With the transporters gone, Ginger suspected that sooner or later those cannons were going to be trained on a target a little bit closer to home.

"We've got to push up," she said, scrambling into a crouched position. "Regroup with Baker. You see the others while you were up there?"

Ghost shook her head. Ginger raised a hand to her helmet and opened a comm channel with the rest of her fireteam.

"Duke? Evans? You hear me?"

She got nothing but static in reply.

"Doesn't mean anything," said Ghost, pursing her lips. "Could be interference, s'all."

"Yeah. You're right." Ginger nodded fervently. "And they know where they're going, same as us. Where's the next point of cover?"

"There's a crashed drop ship; looks like it's from the original scouting party. About twenty-five metres, one o'clock. A fireteam's camped behind it already, but there's room."

"Good. I'm gonna pop a smoke. You ready?"

Ghost flung her rifle onto her back, equipped her submachine again, and gave Ginger a short, sharp nod in confirmation.

Ginger grabbed a grenade from her belt, pulled the pin and lobbed it over their rock. It landed approximately ten metres ahead of their location and promptly began spewing out a thick, grey cloud of smoke. UEC scientists performing autopsies on roaches had discovered that some classes of bug really *did* possess infrared vision, and the latest models of grenade now included a stronger multi-spectrum component in their smoke to mask soldiers' heat signatures, just in case.

"Heads down, eyes sharp," she snapped. "Move!"

They sprinted out from behind the rock, knowing that at any second a new wave of chitin rounds could tear through the smoke and pierce them like pincushions. Ginger gritted her teeth so hard her jaw hurt. Despite her advice to Ghost only seconds earlier, it was tempting to shut her eyes and hope for the best. But she just about kept them open, even when the thick smoke made them sting.

A few puffs of snow burst up around their feet, but both of them made it across to the wreckage of the drop ship in one piece. As Ghost had mentioned, it was already home to a fireteam of marines. The two women hurriedly barged their way into cover beside the group.

"Rogers. Flores. How nice of you to join us."

Ginger pushed her helmet back up her forehead and was surprised to discover Staff Sergeant Baker standing only inches to her left. She didn't recognise any of the other marines, though. They must have arrived in a different transporter.

"Good to see you alive, sir. Didn't know if you made it."

"Of course I did." Baker checked his magazine, then slammed it back into his rifle. "As if I'd be lucky enough to die and finally escape this hell hole."

Ghost scrambled past Ginger, ducking as a hailstorm of bug projectiles ricocheted noisily off the gutted skeleton of the drop ship.

"Have you heard from Duke or Evans, sir?"

"Negative, Private. Last I saw them they were headed down the left flank. No radio contact?"

Ginger's stomach fell. She shook her head.

"Well, if they're alive they know what they need to do. Nothing we can do for them if they're not. Right now, our priority is figuring out how we're going to clear those trenches."

"No roach holes, I'm guessing?"

"Nope. Intelligence screwed up – the only bugs out here are the kind with guns. And they *really* don't want us getting up this hill."

The marine closest to the burnt-out cockpit poked his head over the lip of the window. He jerked backwards a second later, a crater where his face should have been. Everybody cowered as the wreckage was subjected to another endless barrage, even Baker.

"Goddammit," Ginger screamed over the din as she dug herself into the snow. "How the hell did we even get into this mess?"

CHAPTER TWO

(SIXTEEN HOURS EARLIER)

Ginger, better known as Sergeant Elizabeth Rogers by her superior officers, didn't particularly want to attend the day's briefing. At least she wasn't hungover this time.

Things had been quiet the past few weeks. It was apparent that the roaches didn't like the cold all that much, and they certainly didn't travel this far north in numbers that posed a threat to the camps and convoys. After a year spent clearing out bug nests across New Terra, there weren't many marines on base who didn't consider it a welcome respite.

But briefings tended to come hand-in-hand with new orders, and orders rarely ran along the lines of "sit on your arses and do bugger all for a few more weeks," unfortunately.

On top of that, she was pretty sure this was the big one – the operation the past twelve months had been building towards. Command didn't send whole companies out into the great white tundra for no good reason, after all.

Ghost, Duke and Evans stood waiting for her outside the briefing tent. Like Ginger, they were wearing their full thermal gear. Duke even had the furry hood of his jacket raised over his head to keep his ears warm. Everyone had their hands tucked under their armpits to stave off frostbite.

"Jesus, Ginger, what kept you?" Evans may have only joined their fireteam a few weeks earlier when they shipped out from Shen Neu, a recently liberated colony site, but he'd wasted no time growing confident in his new position. "You know I can't pull a trigger if I lose my fingers to the cold, right?"

"That's the plan," Ginger grumbled. "Only way the rest of us can feel safe. I've seen you shoot in target practice."

"Less pissing contest," Ghost said, shivering, "and more getting inside, please."

Duke pulled open the fold of the tent's entrance; the thick fabric rustled and flapped in the freezing gale. They hurried through and refastened the flaps before anyone could complain they were letting the cold in.

More than a dozen plastic, folding chairs were laid out so that they faced an archaic projector system. Christ Almighty. The UEC must have been allocating its fleet an even tighter budget than Ginger realised. Either that, or they were worried about running out of juice so far from the rest of humanity. It was easy to forget just how isolated they were.

At least they had a fire going. The inside was much warmer, no doubt helped by the seven other marines pacing about. One of them was drinking instant coffee from a thermos flask. Dammit. Ginger wished she'd thought of that. She'd passed the canteen on her way there.

No sign of Staff Sergeant Baker yet. He'd be leading the

briefing, as per usual. Ginger didn't know the names of anyone belonging to the other two fireteams. Quite frankly, she didn't really see the point in learning them. It was nothing personal. She just didn't like getting attached to anyone, for obvious reasons. Anyone except Ghost and Duke, of course. And Evans, she supposed, but that was only for the sake of her career.

Bloody hell, it was cold. She crossed the tent to the chairs closest to the brazier and toasted her hands until the last couple of attendees arrived.

"Let's make this brief," said Staff Sergeant Baker, marching in with his data pad tucked under one arm. "I don't want to be out here any longer than you do."

The marines murmured approval. Ginger turned around to face the projector screen and shivered. Everybody else shuffled into their seats as Baker got his data pad synced up.

"Right," Baker sighed. Ginger recognised the weary look in his eyes – he'd clearly spent the whole day in briefings of his own. "So it'll come as no surprise that there is, in fact, a reason we're all out here freezing our gonads off. Yes, ladies, I'm talking to you too. Many of you have no doubt heard the rumours that we've come this far north to blow up some sort of super-nest. Sorry, marines. Close but no cigar."

He tapped his data pad and a picture of an industrial factory projected onto the screen. It was backdropped by a snow-tipped mountain range. Ginger leaned forwards.

This was new.

"Command picked up this facility during their initial scans of the planet," Baker continued. "We believe it was built by the indigenous population in order to mine and process copper, iron and tin more efficiently."

"It's way more advanced than any of the settlements

we've seen so far," said a sergeant from one of the other fireteams.

"They must have been on the cusp of their own industrial revolution," Duke said, scratching his stubbly jawline.

"Command's thoughts exactly," Baker agreed. "There doesn't appear to be another structure like it anywhere on New Terra."

"But why do *we* want it?" Ginger asked. "It's still a relic, even by UEC standards. It can't be of much strategic use, either."

"We want it because the bugs want it. Intelligence can't figure out why they've chosen to infest it, but they must have their reasons. Roaches wouldn't journey this far north otherwise."

"So it *is* another nest, then." Private Evans had pulled off his gloves and was absent-mindedly picking at his fingernails. "You want us to get in there and blow it up."

Ginger rolled her eyes. Baker sighed, exasperated.

"Private, you might want to try closing your mouth and opening your ears for once. You never know, you might learn something. Yes, it's a nest of some kind. The question is, *what* kind? Setting off a nuke is hardly likely to get us the answers Command needs."

Baker tapped his data pad. The presentation moved onto the next slide – an aerial shot of the factory and its surroundings.

"This is Operation Iron Nest. We are to capture the facility so that further studies of the infestation can be conducted. Make no mistake, marines. Command has deemed this to be one of the most important stages of the colonisation campaign thus far."

"What's so special about it, sir?" asked Ghost, crossing her arms. "There must be *some* intel you can give us."

"Need-to-know basis, I'm afraid. The first stage of the operation is to clear the area *outside* the facility. You'll be briefed on further steps once a safe perimeter has been established."

Ghost turned to Ginger and Duke with an eyebrow raised. Yeah, Ginger didn't understand why Command couldn't just spill the beans sooner either. Surely the more they knew, the better the odds of them making it to the facility in the first place.

Baker pointed to the display.

"The northern side of the facility is surrounded by a vast mountain range too insurmountable for anyone but the most experienced climbers, and there's an ocean of icewater to the south and east. That leaves only the open snow plains to the west for our approach. Unfortunately, we can't fly in."

Everybody groaned.

"I know, I know. Bug cannons. There are at least three bordering the facility and we've unconfirmed reports there's another somewhere up the mountains. We lost two drop ships getting these images back when we thought the site was deserted."

"No bombardment?" one of the privates asked.

Baker shook his head.

"Not that close to the facility. Command's learnt from its mistakes. One stray shot and the whole place could go up. We can't risk losing it. That's why we're going in the old fashioned way. Ground transporters will get us to the western flank from base and then we'll push forward on foot, clearing the trenches and cannon pits of roaches as we go."

More laboured grumbling from the other two fireteams. Ginger took a deep breath and shrugged.

"Nothing we haven't done a dozen times before," she said, leaning back in her chair. "Come on, guys. How difficult can it really be?"

CHAPTER THREE

Ginger grunted and clutched at her helmet. Part of the drop ship's turbine snapped off as the bugs continued their barrage.

"Got any ideas, sir?" she yelled at Baker. "Because I don't!"

A fireteam from another squad charged past them down the middle of the western flank. Ginger watched as they miraculously avoided being cut down by the stream of chitin rounds only to instantly disappear when an inbound egg sac crashed down on top of them. A geyser of white snow gushed half a dozen metres into the air; a fine red mist rained down again.

Baker swore and raised a hand to the side of his helmet.

"Kimathi, you there? I've got a couple of fireteams pinned down by the crashed... Yeah, that's the one. Bastards won't let up. Can you provide covering fire while we move round to flank them?"

He paused, listening to Staff Sergeant Kimathi's reply.

"Got it," he said, nodding. "Waiting on your signal."

"What's the play, Sarge?" asked Ghost.

"On your feet, marines. Fireteams Papa and Victor are going to provide covering fire while we cross to that rock face on our right, and then we're going to do the same so they can hit the first of those trenches. Get ready to move."

Ginger craned her neck to see where they were supposed to run. A short ridge of blue-grey rock lay about thirty metres from their position, its modest overhang adorned with icy stalactites. No cover in between. Downhill, slightly. They'd better hope Kimathi's marines did a good job of suppressing the gun-toting mutant bugs up top.

Back in the other direction, far on the other side of the advancing (or in most cases, pinned-down) marines, a group of about seven or eight soldiers – barely any bigger than ants from where Ginger stood – set their rifles to fully-automatic and began spraying the nearest bug trench with everything they had. Almost instantly, the rat-a-tat assault on the side of their drop ship dried up.

"Now!" Baker shouted.

There wasn't time to organise themselves, or spread themselves out from one another; everybody sprinted out from behind cover at once. Seconds later, the storm of chitin rounds started up again. That was the problem with the shuffling, trollish mutant bugs. They weren't like regular roaches. You could get their attention easily enough, but you couldn't make them flinch... and you *certainly* couldn't get them to stop shooting and take cover, even when their ghastly, malformed lives depended on it.

Projectiles punctured the snow around Ginger's feet. Ghost faltered for a moment, but Ginger pushed her onwards. They couldn't think, they couldn't hesitate. All they could do was run and pray they stayed one step ahead of the bugs' aim.

The marine to Ginger's left screamed as a two-inch long

shard of chitin tore through her forearm. It missed the bone but got stuck in her flesh, jutting out both sides like a macabre piercing. Much to Ginger's admiration, the marine grabbed hold of the wounded limb with her better arm and kept on running.

Another soldier wasn't so lucky. A round lodged halfway through his neck. He stopped, clawing at the hole in his throat while coughing up blood. Another shard punched into his ribcage, and then a third into his heart.

There was no helping him – he was already dead. Ginger shoved Ghost towards the cold wall of the ridge and then dived in behind her. All of the other marines made it across in one piece, including the woman cradling her injured arm. Her squadmate already had his med kit at the ready.

"Kimathi?" Baker was on comms again. "We made it across. One dead, one wounded. Yeah, about that. Not sure how great a vantage point we have on them from here. Suppressing fire's gonna be tough."

Even out of sight, the bugs in the trench up top continued to pummel their ridge with projectile after projectile. Some made it as far as the disturbed blanket of thick snow through which they'd run. Ginger tucked herself against the wall of rock and watched as the wounded marine's comrade used a pair of tweezers to pull out the shard. A jet of blood sprayed out; they hastily put pressure on the wound and wrapped a thick bandage around her arm. It wasn't a tidy job, and fragments of chitin no doubt remained inside, but it would do until she could get herself to a proper field medic.

"Right," Baker continued. "That's good. We'll stay put and keep their attention. Radio in if you need us."

The consistent assault from the bugs caused one of the

icy stalactites running along the top of the ridge to crack and fall. It stabbed into the snow between Ginger's legs. She reached up and smashed off the rest with the butt of her rifle, just in case.

"With all due respect, sir," Ghost moaned, "I don't think our situation has improved much."

"Well, you'd be wrong. With the bugs' focus on us, fireteams Papa and Victor can make a break for the trenches. You know how it goes, Private. Incremental gains."

"Tell that to Fedorov," muttered the marine with the wounded arm, staring back at the corpse with a hole in his neck.

Baker crouched with his rifle at the ready, listening to the endless thudding of projectiles hitting the top of their ridge. It was hard for Ginger to gauge how much older Baker was than her. Ten years? Fifteen? He'd grown so many worry-lines and crows-feet since they touched down on the planet. Whatever the answer, he was clearly more experienced than the rest of them when it came to combat. He'd probably served to quell the *first* round of riots back on Earth. Always thinking of the next move – she could do well to learn a thing or two from him.

Eventually the barrage stopped. The cold, wet wall of grey-blue rock ceased quaking and the remaining stalactites no longer threatened to snap off. Everyone waited for a fresh wave to hit them, but it never came. They could hear screaming and explosions and rifle fire further down the line, but, aside from the wounded marines' muffled groaning, their side was totally quiet.

"The mutants must have moved further down the trench," Baker said, carefully stepping out of cover. "The other fireteams got in while their focus was on us. Time to move."

Everybody followed suit. The marine with a bandage wrapped around her limp arm tried getting up as well, but Baker waved her down.

"You stay put and look after yourself. We'll send someone back for you once the trenches are clear. The rest of you, on me."

A little more professionally than last time, they followed Baker out of cover. The ridge wasn't long and it took only a few seconds to navigate around; the hard part was climbing the slope beyond to where the first of the trenches began. The thick snow didn't make the short trip any easier. Ginger's heart jackhammered. Who knew how smart the roaches were, really? Maybe it was a trick. *Maybe* they were just luring what few marines remained out into the open so they could pick them off more easily.

Her eyes snapped from one end of the tiny hilltop to the other. Though the slope couldn't have been more than another couple dozen metres in length, it looked like it went on forever. The crisp snow on the ground melded seamlessly with the ghostly white of the morning sky. She was prepared to throw herself against the ground at a moment's notice should an ugly mutant bug's head break the divide.

Then suddenly the world split into ground and sky again, and a network of earthy pits and furrows stretched out before her. In the split-second before Ghost could grab her arm and throw her forward, she spotted a brief glimpse of the dark, industrial factory in the distance.

"Get inside," Ghost screamed, "before something takes your head off!"

They dropped into the trench alongside Staff Sergeant Baker and what remained of the other fireteam. It was crudely dug using claws and mandibles rather than equipment, a feat doubly impressive once Ginger considered how hard the frozen soil was. It *looked* clear of bugs – even dead ones – but the screams and gunfire coming from further down said otherwise.

"We're gonna be mostly dealing with the mutant breed, it seems," Baker whispered. "Make sure you've all switched to explosive rounds."

As if everyone present hadn't equipped them from the start. Still, Ginger quickly glanced at the magazine in her rifle to confirm. You couldn't take down a mutant with regular ammunition – not unless you had a dozen marines and a good ten minutes to waste, at least – but a few solid blasts to the head would do it. They were shambling, unnatural freaks – anomalies amongst the roach horde.

Ghost instinctively moved to the back of their group. It wasn't cowardice. Her rifle was of the sniper variety, and no-scoping bugs from three feet away wasn't exactly ideal.

"Remember to check your corners," Baker said, leading them forward. "And clear your shots before you take them. Try not to blow your brothers and sisters' heads off."

Ginger could barely keep her rifle steady. Regardless of how many operations she was a part of, going up against the bugs and roaches grew no less petrifying. There was something about the way they scuttled about that unsettled her, no matter how proficient humanity had become at crushing them under its boot.

The trenches – more like shallow ditches, really – didn't follow a set grid. They wormed their way around the hardest of rocks and snaked back towards the factory at weird and random angles. Baker led them as straight down the line as he could, towards the combat, hoping to assist the fireteams who'd attracted the bugs' attention.

A roach scuttled out from a tunnel to their right; the tunnel was tiny, barely big enough for even the bug to fit through. Ginger jumped, but enough of the marines caught sight of it before it could attack anyone. Their explosive rounds blew half of its limbs off before detonating its bulbous head.

They came across a pair of mutant bugs only a few seconds later. They were as ugly as ever. Their faces were twisted into agonised scowls, their features blending together like candle wax left next to a fire. Throbbing tubes ran from their oxen chests, down their thick, carapaced arms and into biomechanical firearms that sprouted where their hands – or at least claws – should have been. Both of them roared senselessly as they sprayed the endless supply of chitin rounds generated in their chest cavities down towards the far end of the trench. In the small gap left between their swollen bulks, Ginger could just about spot a group of marines attempting to return fire.

Baker gestured with hand signals for everybody to get into position. Ginger crouched down at the front beside Baker; the two marines from the other fireteam remained standing with their rifles held out above Ginger and Baker's heads; Ghost retreated slightly, climbed up onto the bank on the side of the trench so she could see over the top of everyone else, and trained her sniper rifle on the mutants.

"Open fire!" Baker cried.

Ginger always thought she was fairly quick on the trigger, but nobody was as quick as Ghost. The first of their explosive rounds had yet to hit either one of the mutants when a shot from Private Flores tore through the back of the skull of the left bug. It staggered forward, not quite dead. A couple of quick shots from Ginger's rifle blew the gory wound out further, finally destroying what little excuse the creature had for a brain.

The other mutant managed to turn around, growling in

uncomprehending fury as round after round blew chunks out from its arms and torso. One of the nauseating tubes running out from its chest burst and a dust cloud of brittle, semi-formed chitin lumps poured out from the flaccid ventricle. One deadly arm was disabled, at least, but that still meant it had another. And crouched up front, Ginger knew she'd be the first to get hit.

She squeezed the trigger and put everything she had into erasing the mutant bug's face from existence. The snarling, warped mouth blew out wider. The eyes were next to go, rendering the monstrosity blind. It raised its arm and sprayed projectiles out across the battlefield before a few more shots from Baker and the others sent its eviscerated corpse crashing down onto the floor of the trench.

"Jesus Christ," Ginger gasped. "I'll never get used to how much damage one of those bastards can take."

"Something's wrong with them, for sure." Ghost hopped down and rejoined Ginger up front. She kept her submachine gun pointed at the two corpses. "No thinking, no feeling. They're more like living, breathing machines than insects."

"Let Intelligence worry about what they are," said Baker, gesturing for everyone to continue forward. "The two of you just need to concentrate on killing them, got it?"

Ghost shrugged and jogged past him.

"Whatever you say, sir."

They paused at the next junction to let Fireteams Papa and Victor advance first. Judging by their numbers, they must have lost a couple of marines either taking the trenches or alighting the transporters. Baker and Staff Sergeant Kimathi shared a brief and exhausted nod as they passed one another.

"Ginger?" said a familiar, booming voice from around the corner. "Ghost? Thank God you're still alive!"

Ginger spun around to discover Duke marching down the trench with Private Evans in tow. He wrapped his colossal arms around Ginger and gave her a brief slap on the back, then did the same to Ghost. Evans offered them a curt nod. A thin but raw scratch ran across his cheek.

"We knew the two of you weren't dead," said Ghost, laughing.

"Sure," said Ginger, winking. "Didn't entertain the idea for a second."

"It was a damn close one, getting out of that transporter," said Evans, shaking his head. He pointed to his cheek. "Got clipped. Got lucky too, I s'pose."

"The bugs were mostly too busy shooting at you to care about us," said Duke. "Mostly. Didn't seem smart to try and follow. Got stuck pushing up the left flank instead."

"Well, we're back together now," Ginger said, giving Duke an affectionate smack on the arm. "No harm, no foul. Save for Evans's face, I guess."

"Let's keep the reunion short, marines. Sigma, clear out any and all roaches down this left trench; these two and I will take the right. If you come across any cannons still operational, you know what to do."

"Yes, sir."

"Good. Get moving."

They split up as instructed. Already the push through the trenches wasn't half as terrifying as when they first dropped down; Ginger got the distinct impression that humanity's tactic of strength in numbers (plus *some* degree of superior military strategy, she supposed) was once again having the desired effect. Soon after leaving Baker they discovered the body of another mutant. Killing it had cost the lives of the two marines lying in bloody heaps beside the bug, but the job was done.

A roach crawled out from another cubby hole; Sigma paused momentarily to blast its screeching insectoid face across the snow-tipped crest of the trench. Another fireteam charged past the mess above them, far more bravely than anyone could have imagined only ten minutes before. The last of the mutant bugs were presumably either dead or engaged with other units.

Despite the sub-zero temperature, and despite Ginger's impression that the battle was effectively won, a bead of sweat trickled down her temple. Her rifle barrel, like those of her squadmates, snapped from corner to corner, top of each trench to bottom, hole to crumbling hole in search of hidden roaches. They found a couple more scuttling down the trenches – often trying to flee from another fireteam – and dispatched them easily. By this point, they were simply performing clean-up.

"Hold up, Ginger." Duke raised a fist like a bowling bowl. "Bug cannon, nine o'clock."

About forty metres to their left, through a narrow channel of snow and dirt that even Ghost would have had trouble squeezing through, was a wider pit. Ginger could make out the blur of roach limbs and, filling her view beyond that, the squirming mass of one of the slugs the bugs farmed for explosive egg sacs. Had it not been for the unmissable green plume of a sac being catapulted up towards the atmosphere, they probably would have stormed right past it.

Now they'd seen it, however, they couldn't ignore it. The cannon had to be dealt with.

"There's no way we're reaching it through the roach entrance," Ginger said, nodding to the narrow fissure. "We'll have to go over the top. Evans and Ghost, you stay here and make sure no roaches escape. Duke and I—"

"Wait up." Evans casually pointed towards the pit. "I reckon somebody else has got it."

A lone marine, either separated from his fireteam or its sole survivor, charged up through the snow to the edge of the pit and lobbed a grenade inside. The roaches inside spotted him and chittered furiously. But they didn't have time to scuttle after him. The marine threw himself backwards into the snow just as the grenade went off. It destroyed the cannon and killed not just the roaches, but also the imprisoned sac-slug. Its volatile cargo ignited and blew the sunken pit a few feet deeper and wider.

The marine picked himself up, manically checked the pit for surviving bugs, and then continued his run further into the battlefield.

Ghost whistled. "Now *there's* a man on a mission."

Not that there was much mission left. Shortly afterwards, a cheer rose from closer to the outskirts of the factory, sweeping through the trenches and across the tundra in a self-congratulatory wave. The last of the bugs was dead. Well, the last of the bugs they could *see*, at least.

"Thank God for that," said Ginger, straightening up. "Maybe now somebody will tell us what the hell we're supposed to be doing here."

CHAPTER FOUR

Claude Raynor strolled leisurely down the corridors of the *Final Dawn's* residential quarters. Section 5 was cramped, and too cold, and more than a little overpopulated in Claude's opinion – just like everywhere else on the Ark. Well, everywhere except the premium upper-class suites, that is. But that was a whole other world, figuratively speaking. Some things never change, he supposed.

Not that he was complaining, mind. He hadn't forgotten the relief he felt when the *Final Dawn* had finally taken off from Earth. The memory of all those desperate people screaming outside the launch pad while he boarded still sent a shiver down Claude's spine. No lack of thermostat or shortage of leg space in his bunk room would ever outweigh the morbid alternative.

He offered his neighbour a polite nod as he squeezed past two residents who'd decided the narrow, steel-walled corridor was a perfectly reasonable place to stop and hold a conversation. His neighbour, whose name Claude *thought* was Simon, rolled his eyes in good-humoured sympathy. Yes, Simon understood. *Some* people weren't on the Ark just because they were lucky enough to win a bloody lottery ticket. *Some* people had jobs to do in places they needed to be.

Three elevators lay at the end of the corridor. One set of doors was open, but not for long. Two residents stood inside the cabin not talking to one another, waiting for them to close. Claude was sure they could see him fighting to get there in time, but neither did anything to hold the elevator for him. He cursed under his breath. If this was the calibre of human from which their species was supposed to rebuild itself, they really were screwed.

He stuck out his hand and stopped the doors from closing. One of the silent passengers, a fellow in a dark suit who presumably still held onto old-world ideas of gentlemanly work attire, suffered a twitch in his cheek as Claude shuffled in, stoney faced.

Claude reached across and pressed the button for Sector 32, which housed the scientific research labs, and watched through the closing doors as one of his many hundreds of neighbours made a dash for the elevator. Without the slightest sense of irony, he did nothing to help them. *He* had places to be, after all.

The elevator shot off. Hardly an elevator in the literal sense, it travelled horizontally through the ship rather than vertically – each sector was a ring running around the barrel-shaped exterior of the Ark, which constantly rotated like a centrifuge to create a sense of gravity. This meant that "down" was entirely relative to wherever your feet happened to be, and that there was therefore no "up" to which anyone in the exterior barrel could ascend. Elevators either travelled the length of the ship from sector to sector – nose to rear, if you will – or, when travelling from end to end within the same sector, followed the curvature of the ring around like a shuttle. The system took some getting used to. The Arks were around thirty years old – the only part of them that sported the same artificial gravity tech as the UEC battlecruisers was the central column around which the barrel rotated. The elevators connecting the column to the barrel really *did* go up and down, however, often requiring a disorienting switch in perspective halfway, but Claude had never stepped foot in that area. The bridge and high-security divisions were off-limits to all but essential personnel.

Halfway to his sector, Claude checked his data pad. He still had ten, maybe fifteen minutes to spare. He reached back across to the panel and, much to the quiet irritation of the suited gentleman behind him, pressed the button for Sector 19. The elevator rumbled to a stop exactly twenty-eight seconds later.

Claude stepped out into a promenade much wider than the cramped residential quarters of Sector 5. It was much brighter, too. Though the sector followed the same wedding band shape as every other, Sector 19 had been *designed* to look as if its roof was domed. Reinforced portholes in the high ceiling showed a panorama of stars twinkling outside. Planters of real trees, flowers and shrubbery lined the middle of the walkway and were flanked by park benches. Couples strolled hand in hand; children excitedly ran up and down its length. A few small birds even flittered amongst the foliage.

He liked it here. So did everyone else, apparently, which is why it was so damn busy all the time.

Claude strolled along the walkway for a few minutes, savouring the fresh air. Well, not fresh. The carbon dioxide in Sector 19 was about as recycled as everywhere else on the Ark – there was just a lot more of it here than in any of the living quarters thanks to the authentic plant life. The scenery wasn't all he came for, though.

The further along the promenade he walked, the more the commercial district beyond crept over the horizon. He saw neon signs for supermarkets, cafes, restaurants, general stores – even a few boutiques, though most of the passengers on the ship didn't have much in the way of disposable income and new products were hard to manufacture or source. Their doorways lined each side of the promenade whilst smaller stands and tables for outdoor dining filled its middle. A couple dozen delicious odours bombarded Claude, most of which still seemed pretty novel – there hadn't been scenes like this back on Earth for decades.

Most of the stores and eateries operated on a twenty-four hour schedule – or at least, the bigger brand names lining the promenade did – though some were busier than others given it wasn't even nine in the morning yet. Oh-nine-hundred hours ship-time, that is – he'd be damned if he knew what time it was down on New Terra. The Arks and UEC fleet still operated on Earth hours, regardless of the day-night cycle of the planet below.

He passed under a pair of golden arches and leaned against the modest counter of his regular hole-in-the-wall, *Greg's Dark Matter Diner*. Food just good enough to be edible at prices that didn't burn a hole first through his pocket, and then the *Final Dawn's* hull.

"Hey, Claude." The manager, Greg, cheerfully pretended to check his watch. "It's not Thursday already, is it?"

Claude smiled impatiently. A year after leaving Earth, he wasn't even sure what a Thursday was anymore.

"The regular, please. Black coffee and a doughnut."

"Coming right up."

He patiently waited the thirty-something seconds for his

order to be fulfilled. His black coffee came in a sturdy, brown, recyclable cup. There was milk on the Ark – the artificial kind, it wasn't feasible to raise livestock on a starship – but Claude didn't see the point in paying extra for it. Nobody whose budget forced them to buy instant coffee ever drank it for the taste.

Claude watched a clunky robot march down the length of the promenade and shivered. Automata, they called them. Completely sentient, apparently, despite some of them looking like trash cans that decided to take a walk. He didn't know where they came from, but more and more of their kind had started turning up to help ever since the debacle back on New Eden a year ago. He wasn't sure if it was right, trusting something without a face... but at least nobody expected him to work with one.

The doughnut came tucked inside a paper napkin – everything disposable also had to be recyclable so that the Ark never ran out of material. Who knew how long they'd be stuck floating up there? As usual, it was a little stodgy, a little dry – probably baked yesterday. He settled his bill, grabbed both items off the counter and set off back down the promenade, slowing only to check the time on the digital clock suspended from the ceiling.

Almost nine. Crap. Maybe he shouldn't have taken the detour after all.

He was lucky there was a free elevator only a few sectors "down" from his own. Five minutes later, it rumbled into the Sector 32 station. Other employees alighted the shuttles and elevators around him. Luckily, his laboratory was close by; he hurried the short distance as quickly as his sloshing coffee would allow and, momentarily stuffing the doughnut into his mouth to free up his other hand, scanned his keycard to open the security door.

"Claude!" said the young Korean man standing on the other side. "There you are! This is not a good day to be late, you know."

"Relax, Ken." Claude retrieved the doughnut from his mouth and waltzed over to his desk. The office section was where most people worked day-to-day; he could gaze inside the *proper* lab with jealousy through the floor-to-ceiling windows at the back of the room. "It's five minutes. The Ark's not gonna stop turning without me."

Ken lurked beside him as he cleared some room on his desk for his breakfast. Claude wished he'd stop fidgeting. It was making him nervous, too.

"Sure," Ken said, "and you can tell that to Admiral Blatch when she comes down here asking why you've held up the whole Iron Nest operation. You knew you were on call this morning. They're waiting for you right now."

Claude almost choked on a mouthful of scolding coffee.

"Then what the hell are you waiting for? Patch them through!" He hurriedly switched on all his monitors and logged into the ship's intranet. "Somebody could have pinged me, you know..."

Ken rushed back to his own computer a few desks over and connected the video feed to Claude's. Then he rolled his chair over and sat beside him, only half visible in the frame.

The picture came through. It was sharp enough, though nowhere near the resolution expected from a data pad, let alone a desktop monitor. It lost a couple of frames every few seconds, too. Nothing they could do about that, though. The feed was coming in live.

Five faces glared through the screen at them. One man was noticeably older than the others; another was built like one of the forklift trucks down in the hangars; the third had a cut across one cheek that was still bleeding. The two women, though. Jesus. They looked about ready to stab him in the jugular. Claude sure wouldn't want to be the guy hitting on *them* in the Star Lounge.

What the hell reason did they have to be so miserable, anyway? They spent their days in the great outdoors, not working seven-day shifts in a sterile office. They slept under the stars, not in a cold bunk the size of a damn coffin. Cry him a river, why don't they.

"About bloody time," the oldest marine snapped. "Do you realise the losses we suffered to make this call happen?"

"Sorry, connection issues." Claude subtly nudged his doughnut out of view. "Temp satellites. You know how they get."

"Just tell my damn troops why they're here," he grunted, stomping out of shot. The remaining fireteam eyed Claude expectantly, their stoney expressions unchanged.

"Right," Claude spluttered, bringing up all the files associated with the Iron Nest operation on his monitor. "So, there's this facility, and—"

"We know about the facility," the female marine in charge sighed, rolling her eyes. She sat forward and jabbed a thumb over her shoulder. "We can see it. It's right there. What do you boffins want us to *do* with it?"

"Of course, of course. Erm, you're a recon fireteam, yes?"

"Last time we checked."

"Right. Well. To cut a long story short, there's something different about the nest under this facility. Maybe it's something we missed in the other nests, maybe it isn't. Hard to say for sure. We've been blowing them up when we should have been studying them."

The marine with a sniper rifle scoffed.

"Study them?" she said, smirking. "Come down and try. I

give your white ass thirty minutes before you head back to orbit."

"Yes. Well." Claude cleared his throat. "Be that as it may, Command wants a fireteam to infiltrate this nest and collect samples. We have a hypothesis regarding where some of the roaches came from, but we need data. Before we wipe them all out, preferably."

The big marine shrugged his not inconsiderable shoulders.

"So, what?" he said. "You want us to, like, scrape the gunk off the walls, or something?"

Claude sighed. His coffee was getting cold.

"You've seen some of their gestation sacs, yes? When you've gone into nests to set off charges, I mean. Ideally, we'd like you to haul a whole cocoon up to the surface for monitoring, but your superiors tell us that's not an option. So I want you to open one up and carve off a sample instead. A suitable receptacle has been provided."

"And then what?" asked Sergeant Rogers. "We just leave?"

"I shouldn't have to reiterate how important a viable sample could be for understanding the bug threat," Claude insisted. "It could completely unlock the secrets of their biological hierarchy." He waved his hand dismissively. "Once the sample is secure and verified, you can do... well, whatever it is you normally do. Nuke it like all the rest, I imagine."

"What else are we good for, right?" Sergeant Ginger looked at somebody standing behind their screen. "I think we're done here, sir."

The video feed shook as if someone was fiddling with the camera, and then cut out. After a tense moment waiting in vain for the comms to reconnect, Ken pinched the bridge of his nose and let out a pained whine.

"You know what?" said Claude, taking a bite out of his doughnut. "All in all, I think that went pretty well."

"WHAT A COLOSSAL TOSSPOT," said Private Evans.

"You can tell he's been off-world too long," Ginger added, standing up from the crates they were using as stools. "Still, we've got our orders. Seems simple enough. Probably won't be."

"Damn right it won't." Staff Sergeant Baker instructed one of the technicians in the temporary command tent to pack the communication equipment away. "Those cocoons are located deep below ground. You'll likely have to shoot your way through a dozen swarms to get anywhere near them. Getting an uncontaminated sample while all that's going down? Ain't gonna be easy. Oh, and it gets worse."

"Of course it does," Ginger groaned. "What else?"

"The bugs knew we were coming. Seems obvious when saying it out loud, I suppose, but all of the regular entrances to the factory are blocked. Whatever's down there, they really don't want us getting in and finding it."

Duke shrugged.

"Can't we just, you know…" Duke mimed an explosion with his hands. "Make a *new* entrance?"

"And risk blowing up the whole facility? No way. Major Liu would court martial us. It'll take some time to cut our way through that weird, crunchy gunk they've plastered all over the factory exterior, but we'll get it done. We just won't get it done quick enough. We all know the bugs can be smarter than we give them credit for. If they figure out what we're after..."

"They might destroy their own cocoons just to spite us," said Evans, catching on. "Bollocks."

"So, what?" Ghost turned around to squint at the factory's imposing black exterior. "I take it you don't expect us to sit back and hope the bugs play nice."

"Of course not." Baker marched past Ghost and pointed up towards the mountains behind the facility. "We just had to find you a different way inside."

Ginger, Duke and Evans stomped through the snow after him.

"Why do I feel like I'm not going to like this?" she asked.

"Because you don't like anything, Sergeant Rogers. At least it'll keep you moving, something that can't be said for all the poor sods who'll have to stand guard outside. This whole sorry operation's a damn frostbite risk..."

"The plan, sir?" Duke asked.

"Ah, yes. Our satellites picked up a trail leading up the mountain. Not the whole way," he added, noticing everyone's faces drop. "The path goes up past the factory's roof. You should be able to get inside through one of the vents in the upper chimneys, providing you get there before the roaches seal those up too."

He beckoned over the technician from before. They hurried out from the tent with a translucent container clutched protectively in their gloved hands. It was about the size and shape of a large thermos flask.

"One of you needs to take this," Baker continued. "Try not to contaminate it, will you?"

"On it," said Duke. He took the receptacle and clipped it onto his belt. It dangled precariously amongst his grenades.

"Don't bugger this up, Sigma." Baker sighed and shook

his head. "It won't just be your arses on the line if you fail. This has been a long twelve months, but we're almost done. Get through this and maybe us frontliners can start building a new world instead of just destroying the old one."

"Yes, sir," Sigma replied as one.

"That's what I like to hear," he said, allowing himself a wry smile. "Now restock your ammunition and wrap your thermals up tight. You've literally got a mountain to climb."

CHAPTER FIVE

Ginger couldn't believe the world could get any colder, but the higher they climbed, the more frigid the air became. It was the antithesis of how the asphalt back on Earth had absorbed the sun's terminal heat as the day went on; the mountain hoarded the frost, grew stronger off it.

Not that Sigma had to trek all that high, luckily. Though the sheer, craggy mountain was itself intimidating, the trail rose barely a hundred metres up the side of the closest peak. The harsh gradient of the ascent did little to warm their muscles as they climbed, however. The issue, Ginger realised, was that they were increasingly exposed to the elements.

"I don't see," wheezed Private Evans, "why we couldn't... just wait for the damn doors to be cleared."

"We ain't letting the bugs dictate our next move," Duke replied, puffing out his cheeks with exhaustion. "We're a recon unit. It's our job to go in first."

"Just don't see what can be this important," Evans said with a shiver, "that's all."

Ginger would have rolled her eyes, but she feared they'd

already frozen in place. She wished she could tuck her gloved hands underneath her armpits to keep them from turning into popsicles, but she needed them outstretched for balance. Gritting her teeth to stop them from chattering would have to do.

"Focus on the trail," she grunted. "It'll be warmer once we get inside."

"We hope," Ghost muttered.

The wind whipped at the fur-lined hoods of their coats and pulled at the straps of the rifles slung over their shoulders. Ginger wished they'd been issued with the snow goggles usually distributed to advance recon groups in tundra regions; it took all of her resolve not to shut her eyes against the stinging gale. Not that keeping them open made much difference. Everything ahead of her was a swirling blend of blue and white; it was near-impossible to tell whether she was walking over icy rock or sky.

She looked back down the trail. Though they'd only been walking for about half an hour or so, the marines busying themselves down in the UEC's makeshift base already looked like the figures generals used to move around the old maps of battlefields, though in this case they'd been stationed atop a white kitchen tablecloth. With her back to the mountain range, Ginger could stare far across the empty expanse of snow across which their transporters came. Perhaps there was a snowstorm on the way; perhaps there truly wasn't anything else out there for miles around. To her left, over on the other side of the black, industrial factory, lay the iceberg-laden ocean. Judging by the large waves crashing against the biting, crescent-shaped shore, the sea was being battered by the same winds as the exposed mountainside.

Ginger only realised she'd stopped walking when Duke

gave her a couple of pats on the shoulder as he passed by. She pulled the lip of her hood further over her helmet and continued trudging upwards.

"What do you think they expect us to find with this, anyway?" The receptacle on Duke's belt was large enough that it stuck out from his coat; Evans reached across the trail and gave it a flick like a nurse preparing a needle. "Some sort of chemical we can use to wipe out the whole roach army?"

"Watch it," Duke snapped, covering the container up again. "We've only got the one of these."

"Who cares?" Ghost shrugged up front. "It's the job. They ask, we do it. If there's a chance the sample Command wants us to get helps end this war, I'm all for it."

"Sure. Course." Walking against a fresh gale, Evans hunched his shoulders even further. "I'm just curious, that's all. If we *do* help end the war, I want to know how."

"I s'pose that's fair enough." Duke shielded his eyes from the snow with his hand and peered further up the mountain path. "I wonder if Jackson would have known. He was always banging on about bugs having hives and hierarchies, wasn't he? Maybe the poor sod was right."

"God, I hope not." Ghost glanced back at them. "I don't mean to speak ill of the dead or whatever, but let's not forget that prior to getting his head blown off, Jackson could be one hell of a creep sometimes."

"Maybe," said Duke, "but that creep knew his creepy-crawlies. Zoology, or whatever he called it. He would have been perfect for this mission."

"Wait, who's this Jackson guy?" Evans barged his way back into the conversation. "Was he the bloke in Sigma before me? Was I sent here to replace a dead guy?"

"Jackson was never in Sigma," Ginger quickly retorted.

"He was in Tau, but their unit suffered casualties and our two fireteams were temporarily folded together. But he's dead, yeah."

"First we had Sergeant Yates," said Ghost. "A ripper got him back on New Eden, God rest his soul."

"Good man," said Duke, soberly.

"Then Ginger became Sergeant and Private Bradley joined us for the drop onto New Terra a year back. After him came Müller, and *she's* the one you replaced."

"And *she* died?" asked Evans.

"May as well have," Ginger replied. "Got transferred to Little Brook. Dustball town in the arse end of nowhere. She'll lose her mind long before a roach gets her."

Ghost kept silent, Ginger noticed.

They continued trekking upwards, their boots crunching through the untouched snow. It lay three or four inches thick, deeper along the edges, the trail shielded from a worse blanket by the overhanging rock face to one side. It was better than a path of pure ice, Ginger supposed, though she found her boots slipping on the rock beneath more than once and none of them had been issued with climbing hooks should the route grow any steeper.

The mountain must have heard her thoughts, or maybe it simply caught her daydreaming, because not a second later Ginger's foot skidded out from under her. She flailed her arms out wide, squinting through the whistling snow and trying to grab hold of something – *anything* – but the sloping rock to her left was out of reach and there was nothing to her right save for a long drop through empty air.

Someone grabbed her arm before she could tumble any further. Ginger turned her head to discover Evans holding on tight, his face beneath his hood contorted with the strain of pulling her back onto solid ground. He succeeded, no small thanks to Duke backtracking and yanking them both away from the edge.

"Cheers," Ginger said, catching her breath. It wasn't an easy job, given how eagerly it whipped away from her.

"Don't mention it," said Evans, distractedly wiping away the beads of frost crystallising around the thin cut on his cheek.

"I wonder what happened to Bradley," Duke mused as they pushed on, a little more slowly this time. "I miss that little guy."

"I still can't believe the lucky bastard made it out," said Ghost, who'd pulled back to let Duke take the lead. "Hell. I can't believe he even survived the first drop."

"When you think of all those marines who died during that first month, it is pretty remarkable." Ginger eyed the peaks; visibility was bad enough, but now the wind was playing tricks on her. She could have sworn she heard a growl; earlier, a screech. "They never should have signed him up to begin with."

"I think of him sometimes, sitting up there in his luxury *Final Dawn* suite sipping from a glass of vintage, Earth-fermented red, and you know what I wonder?"

"I don't know, Ghost." Duke huffed up the slope ahead of her, one of his large hands outstretched before him. "Please enlighten us."

"I wonder what would have happened if Bradley never drove clear of Rhinegarde. Like, if he got caught by one of the hive explosions or the roaches got his truck, or something. When the suite Bradley was waiting for became free, would it have just, like, stayed empty? Forever? Seems a waste when there are millions of us grunts down here who could take it."

Evans laughed.

"Maybe if you prove yourself today, Command will give you a first class ticket next time one of those rich old sods pops his clogs. You'll spend all but a week up there before they start shipping everyone back down to the surface."

"The regular citizens, maybe," said Duke. "They ain't gonna bring any of the wealthy folk planetside until the condos get built, trust me."

"Condos," Ghost grumbled. "We risk our lives and the best *we* can hope for is a damn tent."

"Everybody stop," said Ginger, raising her hand.

"Eh?" Evans peered back at her through the swirling snow. "What now?"

"Shut up," Ginger ordered. "I think I heard something."

They paused and listened to the wind. It howled between the jagged rocks and hissed through crevasses in streams. Their hoods fluttered like pirate sails. A clump of snow grew too heavy up the trail ahead of them and crumbled loose with a sluggish *kerumpf*.

No sounds save for the mountain.

Keeping her hand raised for silence, Ginger inspected the path behind them once more. The way back may not have been completely overwhelmed by the growing snowstorm, but visibility had decreased to such a point that she could no longer make out the camp below. Perhaps it was only the shouting of marines she heard, drifting up the mountain after her. Perhaps she hadn't heard anything at all.

Conversely, the factory was closer than ever. Snippets of its black chimneys loomed through the shifting veil of white. There was no way of telling if their path would take them directly to the rear of the building, or meander around the peaks and ridges before reversing back on itself. But the factory was dead, derelict and, apart from the bugs, deserted. No sound should have been coming from there, either. It must have been the wind again.

Command was counting on them. They had to keep moving.

Besides – if the roaches didn't get them, frostbite would.

"All right," Ginger said slowly. "Keep your guard up. We must be—"

A muffled boom further up the mountain range cut her off. There was no mistaking the noise for wind this time. All four members of Fireteam Sigma jumped and scrambled to pull their rifles off their backs. Their hands were slow from the cold. The loose rocks shifted beneath their feet.

The source of the mysterious noise was revealed seconds later – a soft, green glow rose up from behind the jagged peak beyond their path and continued to soar until it was lost in the ghost-white sky.

Egg sac. Bug cannon.

The mountain caught up with the roar of its launch; Sigma felt the aftershock punch through the rock, watched as a hooked outcrop snapped off and smashed against the slope as if it were as fragile as a dropped vase. Ginger turned her attention to the sounds of crunching and crumpling. Snow was hurrying down the side of the mountain towards them – not quite an avalanche, but more than a big enough landslide to sweep four bone-cold marines off a cliff.

"Backs to the wall, now!"

She barely got the words out before the white torrent reached the foot of the rock face above them. Everybody pinned themselves against the exposed blue-grey ice, though it was probably a fool's hope – the lip of the slope jutted fewer than six inches out over their heads. They were still very much exposed.

The snow crested above them before crashing down

over their narrow trail. Some of it smacked into Ginger's helmet; the majority battered her shoulder. She was glad not to have ducked her head down as instinct first told her – judging by the ache in her shoulder, the force may well have snapped her neck if she had.

There was too much white and nothing else – it was impossible to tell how much of the snow was rushing past them and how much was smothering the path. Ginger didn't dare move her feet to find out. She tried gripping the cracks in the rock as hard as she could, though the ice made her fingers slide right back out again.

She heard a groan beside her. One of frustration rather than agony, thank God. She traced her hand along the rock wall – slowly, in case she accidentally reached into the snowfall and got carried away by it – until her glove brushed against something soft and padded. Her hand was quickly gripped by someone else's – Ghost's, Ginger guessed from its size.

And then, as quickly as it began, the deluge was over. The last clump dropped lazily over the crest in front of them, and all was silent and still, save for the gentle swirl of snowflakes and the mournful melody of the whistling wind.

"Everyone all right?" Ginger asked, before coughing from the sudden chill that flooded her lungs.

"My shoulder's buggered," Evans replied through gritted teeth. "Still breathing, though."

Ghost gave Ginger a curt nod and let go of her hand. Duke stomped past them – the unexpected deluge of snow *had* built up over their trail, but only came halfway up their shins – and grabbed Evans's arm before he knew what was coming. With a hearty twist, Duke snapped it back into its socket.

"Jesus *bloody*..." Surprised, Evans gave his shoulder a

wiggle. "Huh. Cheers, mate, I guess. Maybe give me a bit of warning next time, yeah?"

Duke gave him a slap on the shoulder. The bad one.

"You're welcome."

"That was a bug cannon," said Ghost, just in case anyone else present hadn't figured it out yet. "We've got to clear it out."

"No," said Ginger, shaking her head. "We don't. Command knows there are bug cannons up in these mountains – that's why they didn't send any more drop ships in after the first fly-bys failed. Our orders are to follow the trail up to the chimney vents and get this sample. No deviation from the mission, no matter what. Understood?"

Everybody nodded and grunted their approval.

"Good. And cut the chatter. There are roaches in these ridges – let's not bring *them* down on top of us, too."

CHAPTER SIX

The trail narrowed further, at its thinnest point stretching only a few feet across, and the angle of ascent grew more severe. When they approached the stage where the only way forward was to climb on all fours, Ginger started to suspect something wasn't right.

"Christ Almighty," said Evans, bringing up the rear. "We've been walking for ages and the factory seems as far away as ever."

Ginger couldn't argue with that. Though it had likely been no more than an hour since they started their trek up the mountain trail, their briefing via satellite link felt like days ago. Someone had made a mistake. Either Command had underestimated how long it would take a fireteam to navigate the route up to the chimney stacks, or Sigma had made a wrong turn somewhere.

Ginger's heart started hammering. This was not good.

"Bollocks." Duke pointed down the side of the mountain. "That's where we ought to be, I reckon."

A second – not to mention far more defined – trail ran across the side of the mountain about twenty metres below their position. It was only possible to see it now that the snowstorm had abated slightly. The rocky, snow-swept slope bridging the two paths wasn't quite a sheer drop, but it wasn't far off, either.

"Yeah, I think you're right." Ginger sighed and shielded her eyes from the sun; its glare reflected off almost every surface she looked at. "Goddammit. Where the hell did the path split?"

"Beats me," said Ghost. "Are we sure the path doesn't loop back on itself further ahead?"

"I'm not even sure we're *on* a path anymore," said Evans, kicking the loose pebbles beneath his feet. "We've been walking far too long, guys. I told you it would've been quicker to wait for them to cut open the doors…"

"What's it gonna be, boss?" Duke stepped back from the edge of the trail and turned to Ginger. "Keep going, or turn back?"

Ginger wiped a clump of snow off the top of her hood while she desperately tried to figure out her answer. This was supposed to be a simple infiltration job, goddammit.

"I don't fancy trying to head back down that path, do you?" Nobody disagreed; trying to navigate their way down some of the steeper slopes amounted to suicide. "Besides, Command will court-martial us if we end up trekking all the way back to camp. Best push forwards."

"Can always blame the delay on weather conditions," said Evans, shrugging. "If we don't slip and break our necks, that is."

Ginger squinted out at the clear sky as she tried to get her bearings. At least the factory was in clear sight, even if it didn't feel as if they'd grown any closer. The camp was almost invisible, still shrouded by the same cloud of light snow which had plagued their ascent, though she could make out a few individual marines, plus what looked like a truck-mounted drill of some kind, travelling to and from the base of the industrial building. The waves of the icy sea were no less fierce than before; the same cold wind stung her cheeks.

A small, bird-like creature caught her eye as it crossed over the pale, cloud-smothered sun. A black silhouette, its wingspan could have been no more than a couple of feet from tip to tip, and its short beak was curved like a coat hangar. It was alone; no flock followed it from behind the peaks.

Ginger watched it turn lazily on its axis as it glided perhaps twenty or thirty metres from their position standing atop the precarious ridge. She was surprised to see anything indigenous living this far north, in all honesty. Perhaps the seas provided more sustenance for wildlife than the land.

But no sooner had she turned back to the trail, a second shadow swept across the rocks and snow, quick as a strike of black lightning. Its smoky shape billowed outwards and then suddenly the small bird was gone, only a sharp flurry of blood and feathers to mark its death.

Ginger let out a surprised cry and staggered backwards, further distancing herself from the others. At first she was convinced it was another of the giant pterosaurs she spotted gliding over the tropical rainforest vistas of New Eden. It wasn't, of course. Wrong planet. As the predator emerged from the glare of the sun, violently shaking shards of bone and tufts of feathers from its maw, its wiry frame came into focus.

Not a pterosaur, then. Something much worse.

"Flying roaches," she muttered to herself. Realising none of the others had seen it yet, she raised her voice beyond a whisper. "Flying roaches! Move, goddammit. *Move!*"

The hoods belonging to the rest of Fireteam Sigma shot up. Their rifles followed shortly after. Luckily, Ginger caught up and ordered them to stand down before anyone could fire.

"Don't shoot, you idiots!" She gesticulated aggressively down the trail ahead. "We know there's a bug cannon up here. Now we have good reason to think there's a whole nest. Do you really want to bring the lot of them down on top of us? Or the whole mountain, for that matter?"

They inched forward up the path with their weapons at the ready. Evans and Ghost trained their rifles on the flying roach taking a long sweep around their position; Duke watched the steep trail ahead with his shotgun attachment primed to fire; the barrel of Ginger's rifle twitched from one snow-tipped rock to another. Their steps were slow, the crunch of the snow muffled. The rest of the path, deserted.

It didn't appear to have noticed them. Roaches weren't exactly subtle creatures. With any luck it would glide right past, none the wiser.

They only got about half a dozen metres further up the ridge before Fate shot them in the foot. A canopy of snow chose that moment to fall from one of the few trees reaching out from the side of the mountain like the fingers of frozen climbers. Nothing to do with Sigma; nothing Sigma could do to stop it. But, in the crisp quiet, the snap of the tree's brittle branches was as loud and clear as any gunshot. The roach was too far away for Ginger to see it turn towards their squad, but none of them mistook its screech.

"So much for stealth then," Ginger grumbled deep in her throat. "Ghost, you got it?"

Private Flores readied her sniper rifle and knelt down on the pebbled trail. With all her bulky equipment and thermals, it was harder than it should have been.

"Ghost," Ginger said, a little more urgently this time, "do you have it?"

"Of course I've got it," Ghost hissed through gritted teeth. One eye was glued to the backend of her scope. "Just calculating distance, wind speed..."

Ginger turned as steadily as she could; where the sun gazed, the trail turned slick. Her stomach grew as cold as the ice crystals forming on her eyebrows. The was no mistaking it – the roach was screaming through the air towards them. It was getting so close, she could see its mandibles furiously clacking against one another in anticipation of its upcoming meal.

"Ghost..."

Private Flores let off a single shot – not because she felt pressured into shooting, Ginger was certain, but only because it was precisely the right moment to fire. The closer the roach got, the less Ghost had to calculate trajectory and the easier a target the roach became. And she was right. Her fifty-calibre round crossed the windswept gulf in an instant, near enough splitting the incoming bug in two.

The shot was loud, though. Ginger spun around expecting an avalanche to come crashing down towards them, but the mountain's only retaliation was a light snowslide twenty-something metres back along the way they came. What was left of the roach fell into a deep crevasse. All was quiet – quieter, suddenly, than it had ever seemed before.

"Good job," Ginger said in a hushed and hurried tone. "Double-time it, people. We don't know—"

The ground trembled as a dark cloud rose up from behind the mountain. Belched forth as a volcanic smoke plume, a hundred or more flying roaches grew to blacken the ivory sky. Their wings were buzzsaws, their cries shrill like metal being sheared.

"Yeah." Duke pursed his lips and nodded. "I'm gonna say there's a nest."

"What the hell was Command thinking, coming here?" said Evans, backing away with his eyes wide like a truck's headlights on full-beam.

The swarm writhed and circled as its hundreds of bulbous eyes searched for the source of the gunshot. Ginger wondered if base camp was crapping itself half as much as they were. Perhaps, with the last of the dying snowstorm between them, the marines below expected nothing worse to come their way than thunder.

As if the UEC would ever be so lucky.

"What's the plan, Ginger?" Evans elbowed her in the ribs, his eyes flittering between hers and the flying bugs above. "Jesus Christ, guys. What do we do?"

There was no way they'd make it back down the trail without getting spotted, and the way ahead looked even less promising. Ginger forced herself to stop staring at the endless fountain of roaches and peered over the side of the mountain instead. It was steep but, as she'd noted earlier, not quite a vertical drop.

"Sod the trail," she snapped, checking that the strap of her rifle was on tight. "Fastest way to the factory is a straight shot, anyway."

"Don't be a bloody idiot," Evans replied, stepping away from the ridge. "You don't even know—"

"Know what?" said Duke, hurriedly securing his own kit as he caught on to Ginger's plan. "What's down there? A lot of snow and rock, that's what."

"Better than what's *up* there," Ghost added, "that's for sure."

An arm extended towards them from the insect cyclone, twisting tighter and tighter like a towel being wrung out, fondling the sky. It was now or never.

"Bollocks to this," Evans groaned, joining the others at the edge of the ridge. "I knew I should have stayed on guard duty."

As the four of them crossed their arms over their chests, grabbed the straps on their shoulders and tried not to look *too* far down the slope ahead of them, the drone of the roaches grew noticeably shriller. Ginger didn't need to turn around to know what that noise meant. She just wished they had more time.

"Jump!" she shouted.

Fireteam Sigma hopped over the side of the ridge. Fear kept them rigid. This was good – had they landed more softly, they may have rag-dolled all the way back down to base camp. Instead they hit the snow like sleds, their backs glued to the sheer rock beneath. Something ripped loose from Ginger's kit, but she didn't care. The bugs would take much worse.

She tried peering down past her feet and quickly regretted it. The slope sure *looked* vertical from where she was sliding. All was white save for the black chimneys of the factory. They were coming in fast. Too fast. And the trail below theirs suddenly looked a whole lot narrower than it had from on top of the ridge. Hell, it looked scarcely wide enough to walk on.

Screw walking on it. She had to bloody land on it first.

Ginger stretched her hands out, clawing for purchase and finding nothing. Her palms smacked against small rocks poking out through the fine blanket; it stung, even with her gloves to protect her hands from the cold. Her boots churned the snow too much to see properly. She wondered if she could reach out and grab hold of either Evans or Duke for stability. Come to think of it, she wondered if they were even still ploughing down the slope beside her.

Then suddenly her boots hit something. Ginger's knees buckled and she waited for the next drop to come – disoriented and exhausted, there was nothing she could do to stop it if it did. Then the churned snow in her wake came spilling down over her shoulders, and she realised she was back on solid ground again.

Safe. For the next few seconds, at least.

Ignoring the increasingly loud shrieks from the roaches above, Ginger shook her head clean of snow and checked on the rest of her fireteam. Ghost was standing on the smaller trail beside her, her submachine gun already gripped in her hands, ready to move on. Duke was safely down too, though he had his back pinned to the rock wall behind him and he kept blowing out his cheeks. For the whole time they'd been climbing a mountain, Ginger had quite forgotten Duke wasn't the biggest fan of heights. She guessed he hadn't wanted to say anything.

That was her left. She quickly checked the trail to her right.

Empty.

Evans. Where in Christ's name was Evans?

The answer came tearing down the mountain beside her. She cursed loudly. Scared or not, he should have jumped with the rest of them. Those wasted seconds could spell the difference between reaching the factory and being torn to shreds by a thousand serrated mandibles.

Evans had his eyes scrunched tight. Even if he'd kept them open, it wouldn't have made much difference. A mere second from reaching the bottom, he clipped an outcrop hidden by the recent snowfall. It only stuck out an inch, but it was enough. Evans skimmed clear from the edge of the slope...

...and fell over the side of the trail below.

"Oh, shi—" Ginger scrambled forward. "Evans? Jesus, *Evans?*"

"I can't," wheezed a voice from below, "hold... on..."

Evans had one glove clasped on a precarious ledge of ice a few inches below the trail. The other flailed back and forth uselessly beneath him. It was obvious that if he tried to pull himself up, he'd slip. The ice was dripping. It was a long drop with nothing but sharp rocks to break his fall.

"Give me your hand," Ginger shouted down at him.

"Out of the way," Duke barked, pushing her to one side. Not in rudeness, she knew, just urgency. He crouched down, wrapped his hand around the arm Evans was using to hold onto the ledge, and dragged the private up with an almighty, drawn-out groan.

Ginger grabbed hold of Evans the second Duke lifted him above the edge of the trail and pulled him to safety. Ghost had a tight grip on the back of Duke's jacket in case the big guy toppled over after him. Strong as the sniper was, Ginger wasn't sure anyone would be able to stop *that* train from leaving the station.

Evans scrambled back onto the narrow shelf, gasping for breath as his fingers clawed at the thick ice, his boots kicking against stalactites and empty air. Duke collapsed backwards, his chest heaving even more heavily than Evans's, looking as if he was about to throw his guts up. Ghost shot Ginger a look sharper than any bayonet. They didn't have time for this.

A fresh scream from high above the mountain saved Ginger the job of berating her fireteam back onto their feet.

The hungriest of the roaches splintered off and began a bloodthirsty descent while the rest of their black flock continued to twist through the sky like a murmuration of macabre starlings.

"Run," said Ginger, shoving the rest of her squad down the path. *"Run!"*

They sprinted as fast as the narrow trail would allow, knocking clumps of snow off the edge and slipping in spots where the sparkling teal rock was exposed. Adrenaline kept them running when normally they would have stopped to regain their balance; sheer momentum kept them from losing it. The rear of the factory's topmost roof was only a hundred or so metres away now. Its two largest chimneys reared up like black posts either side of a finishing line, while the rest of the monolith's stone and iron facade disappeared down into the fleecy plains of tundra below.

Slowly, the bright white of the mountain around them turned dark and grey. The roaches drew close.

"Goddammit." Ginger glanced over her shoulder. "We've got incoming!"

The first of the roaches were only twenty or so metres above and behind them, the next half-dozen only a stone's throw further than that. There was no way any of them could cover the remaining distance to the factory on foot before getting overwhelmed by the flying vanguard. And this swarm wouldn't just sting or swat or scratch. Hell, you had the same odds of survival standing in the path of a plasma beam. They bit and ripped and stripped the clothes and flesh from your bones. By the time the last roach in the swarm rushed past, there'd be nothing left of Sigma but a red smear, forever lost in the next snowfall.

Ginger had seen it happen before. It wasn't how she planned to go.

She spun around and, still backstepping along the trail as quickly as she dared, fired a couple of controlled bursts at the nearest roach. She clipped one of its translucent wings and it crashed to the ground, snapping its fragile forelegs. Two more buzzed past it without hesitation before shots from Ghost, Duke and Evans ended their flights early, too.

Three down, a couple hundred more to go.

"We can't take on the whole swarm," Ginger wheezed as they all started sprinting again.

Evans's reply came in the form of blind-firing over his shoulder in a panic. Half a magazine spent without even looking. Ginger hoped his lunacy had at least bought them a few more seconds.

"I might have a plan, boss," said Duke, charging ahead like a six-cylinder snow plough. "Gonna need to wait until we're on the rooftop, though."

"Why?"

"Space."

"Christ. I don't care what it is. If we live that long, just do it."

Thirty metres left. Twenty. The factory was built into the very side of the mountain, and the trail widened as it approached the corner of the rooftop. The rear was submerged in a foot of snow; the remainder glistened a polished, onyx black. The two main chimneys were a good six or seven metres in diameter and built from cobbled rock, similarly dark.

Ginger realised she couldn't tell the blood pumping through her temples from the collective drones of the roaches' wings anymore. But that wasn't the worst thing.

"Erm, guys?" she yelled, firing backwards at the closest bug. "Any idea where the hell we're supposed to go from here?"

Alongside the two largest chimneys was a disorderly cluster of smaller pipes and vents, none taller than a man and some already tainted by rust. Past them, the angle of the rooftop sloped slightly before culminating in a massive drop. There were no doorways or stairwells in sight.

"There," said Ghost, jabbing her submachine gun forward. She always did have the sharpest eyesight. "Chimney on the left. Some sort of grille."

Ginger squinted; adrenaline was tunnelling her vision. Some sort of maintenance access grate, by the look of things. This must have been what Command's drones had spotted. Perfect. Hardly the backdoor entrance they'd been told to expect.

"Duke..." The full swarm had begun its descent now. Ginger stopped short of the chimney and started unloading her rifle at it beside Evans, who was switching out his first magazine for another. "Whatever that plan of yours is, you'd better start bloody doing it."

Duke stopped halfway between Ginger and the chimney to rummage amongst the inventory around his waist, while Ghost hammered on the metal grate.

"It's got hinges," she groaned in frustration, "but it's stuck!"

"Course it is," Ginger muttered.

She fired at one flying roach after another, trusting that each short burst hit its mark. There wasn't time to confirm her kills. Limbs burst off; wings were shredded; bulbous heads exploded in clouds of purple. But there were too many. If even one bug made it through, the whole swarm would.

With a triumphant grunt, Duke pulled a pair of canisters out of his satchel. Ginger risked a glance at them.

"What in the name of all that's unholy are *they?*" she snapped.

"Incendiary grenades," he said, jogging up beside them. Ghost gave up on the grate and returned to spray rounds into the swarm too. "Well, self-igniting phosphorus. Bugs don't like fire."

"Jesus Christ, Duke." Ghost looked appalled. "What the hell are you carrying them around for? Nobody's used crap like that since World War Two!"

"Yeah, well. Nobody's ever been at war with insects before, either."

He lobbed one of the grenades towards the left side of the rooftop; a second later, the other to the right. Each detonated upon impact, first flashing and fizzing a white brighter than any blizzard before rapidly spreading outwards in a fluid ruby inferno. A few of the roaches closest to Sigma got roasted instantly. The rest of the swarm behind fanned out in a confused, angry cloud, searching for another way through to their meals.

"And you were just carrying those things in your kit," Ginger said, shaking her head in disbelief as they rushed back to the grate. "Why?"

"You know, to burn a nest. If we ran into one. Can't go around with a sack of C-4 on me *all* the time."

"Oh, of course not, mate." The growing fire painted the left side of Evans's face red. "Because *that* would be stupid, wouldn't it?"

The bugs were dumb. On their own, at least. Thick as bricks. But put them in a horde and together they seemed to figure stuff out. One by one, and then en masse, they rose up above the wall of flames like flies wafted off a day-old corpse.

Up, up... and over.

"We might want to get that grate open," said Ginger, gawping upwards.

"On it," said Duke. "Stand back."

He pumped the undercarriage of his battle rifle and fired a shotgun slug into each corner of the grille. Its rusted hinges blew out with them, as did any bolts Ghost's rushed inspection might have missed. Duke booted the grate inwards. It clanged forlornly down the dark shaft, past a broken ladder that had twisted loose from the wall.

"Can't climb down," he said, shaking his head. "But it's a long drop."

"You got any better ideas?" Ghost rammed her gun into its holster. "You sure seem full of them today."

The swarm of roaches reared high above the mountain, a thrashing, starving black wave poised to crash down on top of them at any second. Ginger considered firing off a few last shots at it, then gave up. It wouldn't make any difference.

"Better the devil you don't know," she sighed.

They jumped.

CHAPTER SEVEN

(SIX WEEKS EARLIER)

Ginger flexed her fingers around the grip of her rifle and cracked her neck. Standing still for so long was making her stiff.

"Steady," a foreman in the clearing below shouted into a handheld radio. "*Steady*... for Christ's sake, Mr. Gwan, go a bit faster than that. We've got three of these to set down before the end of the day, you know."

Above him, a tower crane slowly lowered a stocky, prefabricated house into position. This was New Durban, the site of a bug nest they'd cleared a good month ago, almost. Sigma had been put on guard duty along its outer wall ever since.

Not as a punishment, mind you. If anything, it was kind of a reward. There weren't any more nests detected in their part of the hemisphere. Not big ones, at any rate. Their work was almost done.

Most of the city had been destroyed in the blast, but that had been expected. It wasn't the old race's infrastructure the UEC was interested in, though efforts had admittedly been made to protect whatever little of the aliens' history remained. It was the *site* of New Durban that mattered – proximity to a natural water source, potential trade routes, clear visibility for miles around. The same reasons the old city had been founded there in the first place.

First they'd established a barricade around the city perimeter. It was simple, cheap, and unlikely to withstand a direct blast from one of the tank bugs... but it would do for keeping out any stray roaches. Then they'd started rebuilding. The simple houses they were laying out in regimented blocks weren't designed to be permanent, though Ginger suspected the poorest of New Terra's future citizens might find themselves living there long after the first skyscrapers went up. But at the very least they'd house the construction teams, engineers and other essential workers while the proper city was slowly erected using the planet's resources.

"Lower," the foreman shouted into his radio. *"Lower..."*

One day she'd have a home too, if she lived long enough. But she didn't want some poxy box in a city. She'd spent too long sleeping in cramped, confined spaces back on Earth and aboard the Ark as it was. She wanted something spacey and lakeside, even if that meant building it herself.

The crane deposited its rectangular cargo with a solid, reassuring *thud*. Dust rose up through the clearing. Ginger sighed and turned back to face the open fields outside the city walls. It was bugs she was supposed to watch out for, not buildings.

A voice came over her helmet's comm unit. It was Duke.

"You there, Sergeant?"

"I read you, Duke. You got something?"

"No, all clear. Just thought I'd check in before I came over."

"What? No. Do not abandon your post, Private."

"I'm not abandoning anything." Ginger could tell Duke

was grinning. "I'm just making my rounds. Don't worry, boss. Private Newman has this section of the wall covered."

"Five minutes." Ginger pursed her lips and tried not to smirk. "Five minutes and then you go back where you belong."

A large hand fell on her shoulder. She jumped.

"Sure thing, boss," said Duke, beaming at her.

"Jesus Christ, man. You're too quiet."

"Wouldn't be much good in a recon squad if I weren't." He peered out at the horizon. "Oh, what a surprise. Your view looks just the same as mine. How's Ghost doing?"

"Why don't we ask her?" Ginger raised a hand to her helmet. "Private Flores, do you read me?"

"Loud and clear, Sergeant."

The closest watch tower to Ginger's position on the wall was just shy of a hundred metres away. A tiny figure approached the side of its box and raised its hand in lacklustre acknowledgement.

"Holding up okay?"

"Oh, yeah. Totally. You know me. Loving life."

"See?" said Ginger, turning to Duke. "She's fine."

"Sure she is," he replied sarcastically. "Ghost's been pissed ever since they shipped Müller off to Little Brook for smuggling contraband. You know they were close, even if she won't talk about it. Poor girl's hurting. How do you think Müller's doing out there, anyway?"

"I mean, if we're this bored here... That three-house town only exists because they reckon there might be oil to drill out there. She must be going out of her damn mind."

"Oil." Duke sighed and shook his head. "I s'pose some things never change."

"I wouldn't worry about it. This is a brand new planet. It'll take us years to ruin it."

The cloud cover above the barren meadows broke and the alien sun shone through. Ginger instinctively shielded her eyes with the back of her hand. After decades of avoiding the sun on Earth, it was hard to shake the association between daytime and death. But then she let herself relax – let the bright, golden rays warm her face.

"You know what?" Ginger smiled. "I don't mean to jinx anything, but I think..."

She paused. Duke looked at her quizzically.

"You think what?" he asked.

"I think the worst is over," she finally sighed. "Now get back to your post."

CHAPTER EIGHT

A moment's free fall; a sudden stop.

Ginger heard other *thwump* noises beside her, milliseconds after her own. She tried opening her eyes, but they stung and she quickly scrunched them shut again. She could move her arms and legs, but only slowly. They didn't appear to be broken, though. In fact, aside from what felt like a slightly bruised coccyx, nothing really hurt at all.

So either she was paralysed and the slow movement of her appendages wasn't actually her own doing, or something had broken her fall.

She fought harder to get up. Something shifted like sand and she managed to wriggle her head free. Clumps of whatever held her down spilled away from her skull and, for a split second forgetting she was now inside the foundry, Ginger imagined she'd tumbled into a pile of snow. It sure didn't *smell* like snow, though.

Then she dared open her eyes again and realised the world was black.

Not snow. Soot.

She'd landed at the bottom of the chimney in a round

pit at least twice as wide as the stack itself. A large layer of black powder blanketed a pile of burnt, brittle residue in its centre – maybe wood, maybe something mined from inside the mountain. The air smelled smoky. The walls were formed of stone and iron towards the top of the chamber, just like they were outside the building, though the rest, which curved upwards in the shape of a laboratory boiling flask, glowed a dull, tarnished, bronze colour – the same coppery material Ginger had seen used to build important structures all across the rest of the planet.

A cough to her right. She turned her head and spotted Duke clambering through the grit and hacking up his lungs. An arm waggled back and forth a few feet from where he precariously stood. He yanked the top half of Ghost free; she stubbornly insisted on uncovering the rest of herself alone.

"Please tell me Evans actually jumped this time," said Ginger, causing them both to flinch with surprise.

"You couldn't get me down here quick enough," said Evans, scrambling around from behind her. He extended a hand. "Come on, love. Let's get you up."

"Call me love again and I'll drown you in the latrines," Ginger grunted, though she accepted his offer of help all the same.

No sooner did Ginger climb to her feet than they heard a screech from up top. They snatched their rifles – none of them had been lost in the fall, luckily – and prepared to fend off the swarm again.

The harsh winter sun beamed down through the grille at the very top of the chimney. Nothing moved, save for the mild trembling of Sigma's rifles. A false alarm, perhaps. Then Ginger spotted it halfway up the shaft – the silhouette of a lone roach stood against the light pouring through their improvised opening. It clicked its mandibles together inquisitively and then scurried out of sight before the rest of her fireteam noticed.

"Okay, we're inside." Ginger lowered both her rifle and her voice. "We continue with the mission as planned. Move out."

The damaged grate lay a few metres down from the pile of soot. They were lucky none of them had landed on it. They stepped over and around its buckled frame gingerly, almost superstitiously, before venturing into the hallway beyond.

Duke took point, as usual. He switched on the flashlight of his rifle, then quickly dialled back the beam's intensity. They barely needed it. And not just because of the light filtering down from the top of the chimney, either. Even spots where sunlight couldn't possibly reach were easily navigable once their eyes adjusted.

Fireflies. Well, obviously not *actual* fireflies. An alien breed with remarkably similar physiology. Ginger had seen them plenty of times before – mostly in the bug tunnels leading down into nests, but also around any native ruins that were especially dark and damp. It wasn't altogether clear whether the species was indigenous to the planet or if the roach horde had brought the fireflies with them, but they weren't a threat. UEC scientists had bottled them, tested them for toxins and radiation, and found nothing. Nothing human science could detect, at least. All the tiny critters seemed to do was light the way.

This time, they had no choice but to follow.

They hovered, almost imperceptible save for their bioluminescent abdomens, sparingly and yet with great effect, over and around the entire factory interior. That which they saw so far, that is. From the chamber at the base of the chimney they entered a long, narrow corridor split into two halves – the left side intended for walking, the right side dedicated to rails on which carts would have once delivered combustible material to the stacks. Sigma spread out across both lanes. This was a bad place to force themselves into a bottleneck.

They passed one of the carts halfway down the hall. It was semi-circular, like the bottom half of a globe. Ginger paused to check inside. Empty, though covered in dust and a fine, sticky, web-like substance. It clearly hadn't been used in years.

"I've never seen anything like this on New Terra before," Ghost whispered.

"No," Ginger replied, "but their copper metalwork is everywhere you look. The bridge, the temple in Rhinegarde, the tower of Sciste – even half the walls in here are built with it. Clearly the species who called this planet home before us knew their way around a forge."

"So did the Romans," said Duke, not taking his eyes off the path ahead. Wind whistled through the chimney behind them. "Hell, so did the Mesopotamians. One of the first Bronze Age civilisations, I think. Took another five thousand years before humanity started building foundries like this."

"Well, most of their towns look more medieval to me," said Ghost. "Stone walls, thatched roofs. They must have been right on the cusp of their industrial revolution when the bugs struck. Though of all places, I can't fathom why they'd decide to build their first factory here."

"Industrial revolution." Evans chuckled without humour. "Listen to you lot. You're talking like the aliens who came before were actually *like* us. They ain't. Or they weren't, rather. And besides, a fat lot of good building a bunch of steam trains or whatever would have done them. Bugs would have still wiped them all out anyway."

"I hate to say it, but Evans has a point." Ginger ground her teeth together. "We're not here to discuss alien anthropology. There'll be roaches ahead. Stay sharp."

The rest of the hallway housed no surprises. Neither did the dark, decrepit bronze stairwell they were forced to navigate at its end. More copper panels bolted together on the walls; the same long pair of rails running from one end to the other and twisting around the stairs; archaic lanterns, their glass shattered and their fires long extinguished. The only sound was that of the thin bronze steps groaning under their weight, which after a while evolved from evoking fear to something akin to relief – if roaches could hear them, they would have come running already. Though that wasn't quite true. There *was* another sound, no more than the last gasp of a dying echo at first. A faint whirring, whining noise that came and went; a series of woeful mechanical shrieks.

UEC drills, Ginger concluded. Of course. The rest of the marines stationed outside the factory were still fighting to break through.

It wasn't distance that muffled the sound of the UEC equipment, however, but the depth of the barrier between them, which Sigma discovered for themselves not long after exiting the winding staircase. Where it ended a much wider hall began, sparse yet no inch without purpose. Though Ginger suspected they were in the factory's entrance, this was no welcome lobby. It appeared to be some kind of cart interchange. About a dozen more sets of tracks and rails were set into the floor or suspended from girders above, winding parallel and across one another before threading deeper into the heart of the facility. A few more bowl-shaped carts lay inert along their length – some abandoned despite being fully loaded with ore, others empty save for cobwebs like before.

"Over there," Duke whispered, ducking under a loop of thick iron chain hanging from one of the tracks overhead. "Looks like the main doors."

Ginger was surprised he spotted them so easily. Little of them was visible. Those slivers she could glimpse revealed the doors to consist of the same black stone as the factory's exterior, crudely chiseled but incredibly hardy nonetheless. The rest was coated in a thick, purple-yellow residue that spread out and latched onto the surrounding floor, walls and ceiling in a hard, globulous web. Ginger couldn't tell if it had grown over the doors or been spat at them.

The closer they approached, treading slowly and carefully over the complicated network of rails as if they might be electrified, the clearer the muffled soundtrack of drilling became. Still, the exterior walls of the factory had to be damn thick. Ginger couldn't even hear the voices of her fellow marines on the other side.

"Looks organic," Ghost said once they were only a few feet away. She sneered in disgust. "Same exoskeleton crap the bugs use on their cannons?"

Evans reached forward and hesitantly rapped his knuckles against the alien material the way a young child might knock on the door to their headmaster's office – as if he feared it might actually open.

"Stuff's harder than rock," he said, shaking his head. "Gonna take a bleedin' diamond cutter to break through that."

"Let's hope not." Despite the continuing shrieks of the drill outside, Ginger failed to discern any cracks in the blockage. It seemed the marines on the other side weren't having much luck. "That's our only way back out, remember."

"Speaking of which…" said Ghost, pointing her gun back

in the other direction. "My gut tells me *that's* our way further in."

Down past the myriad of criss-crossing tracks and levers was another hallway similar to the first – one side for walking, the other for transporting ore. There were at least half a dozen of these corridors sprouting out in different directions from the main interchange, each illuminated solely by the tiny fireflies fluttering down its length. What singled Ghost's hallway out in particular was not its design, nor its unknown destination.

It was the same hard, purple-yellow residue plastered across every inch of its dusty walls.

"Yeah, I think you might be right." Ginger gestured Duke forwards. "If we're gonna find this sample, it'll be by following the bugs. Unfortunately."

She raised a hand to her helmet.

"Baker, sir, do you read me? Command, do you read me?"

Nothing. Typical. The sooner the UEC adopted quantum-entangled communication systems that didn't get blocked by something as simple as a thick wall, the better.

"No luck?" Evans raised an eyebrow. "Do you reckon we should hang back, try to get word to them from this side of the barrier? Like, let them know we made it in all right?"

"Nah. When they do finally get these doors open, we're gonna be back here to greet them with the sample in our hands, not twiddling our thumbs waiting for a pat on the back for not dying yet. Understood?"

Evans raised both eyebrows this time.

"Yes, ma'am."

They crossed the tracks and stepped carefully through the hall. Duke and Ghost took the lead; Ginger and Evans guarded their backs. Though roaches weren't ones for patience any more than they were subtlety, she couldn't help feeling like she was being watched. Like something was waiting for them.

She expected the hardened residue to crack and crunch beneath their boots, yet more often she found herself slipping on its waxy, wavy surface. Plastic. That's what it reminded her of. Great dollops of thick, heat-warped plastic. She kept her feet planted firmly on the exposed floor wherever she could.

Ghost was wrong, she thought with a shiver. It didn't feel organic at all.

Duke had to barge open a door that had been left ajar at the far end; it wasn't locked and neither had the bugs tried to block it with their goop, but it grunted with resistance all the same. He stumbled into the room beyond with Ghost in tow, swinging their rifles back and forth as they checked their corners.

"Erm, boss?" He beckoned Ginger inside. "Get in here. You're gonna want to see this."

She stepped carefully through the doorway, clutching her rifle tight just in case Duke was being unusually cavalier about possible threats. When she realised what he was looking at, her arms went limp again.

Two columns of giant smelting pots, linked together by scores of colossal iron chains, were paused midway through their journeys up and down an industrial mine shaft dug two hundred metres into the earth. It was carved straight out of the ice-cold rock, though Ginger couldn't help noticing the walls were now reinforced with a certain hardened toxin. The mechanical system appeared to be designed so that, upon reaching the top of the chain, the pots would pour the ore into funnelled channels leading elsewhere in the factory before heading back down the shaft again. Or they would have, had it been operational. Now it lay still, silent – a machine morgue.

Christ Almighty. The facility was so much bigger than anybody thought.

"What the hell were the old race *doing* here?" she asked, gawping down into the chasm.

"It's a good question," said Evans, "but I've got a better one."

Ginger raised an expectant eyebrow.

"What do the bugs want with it now they're gone?" he offered.

"I guess we're gonna find out," sighed Ghost. "How are we supposed to get down there?"

Ginger searched for another way down. There wasn't a passenger elevator anywhere she could see. Hell, there wasn't even a security barrier around the giant pit. The aliens that came before may have been close to a new Industrial Age, but they were still a long way from establishing proper Health and Safety protocols.

"That crank over there," she said, nodding at a wheel attached to a winch through which one end of the giant chain was threaded. "I'm guessing they used it to lower the pots. There's probably another one at the bottom. Those pots are pretty big. Room for two at a time, maybe. If we can get those chains moving, I reckon we can ride the system down."

"No way." Evans stared at her. "You saw the state of that ladder back at the chimney. This place is falling apart. You're going to get us all killed."

"Not if we're careful. But you know what *will* get us killed, Private? Disobeying orders. Command hates failure, but they court martial those who give up."

She glanced at Ghost and Duke. They looked barely any

more keen to get inside one of the pots than Evans did. But they weren't saying no, either.

"Ghost and I will go down first," she said, nodding to Private Flores. "Duke, work the crank. If it's safe and there's another crank where the shaft ends, we'll bring the two of you down after."

Each pot passed a short platform jutting out over the edge of the pit. One pot, luckily empty, hung only a couple of feet below. Ginger paused at the lip, her vision starting to swim, wishing she could overrule her own orders without compromising her command of the fireteam. She could barely make out the bottom of the shaft. One tiny slip...

She lowered herself into the pot before she could think too hard about it. Maybe this was as dumb a plan as it sounded. But it wasn't as if they had any other choice.

The pot immediately groaned with the added weight. Ginger held out her arms for balance as it swung slightly. She heard a series of deep clunking sounds from somewhere inside the machinery, but the chains held... for now.

Ghost cast her a deadpan look from the edge of the platform.

"Thanks *so* much for volunteering me, Ginger," she said, before carefully climbing down after her.

The chains creaked, the pot swayed, but still they avoided crashing to their deaths. She'd been right to assume two passengers was each pot's maximum capacity. When it was clear the worst wasn't about to happen, Ginger nodded to Duke. Then she grabbed the rim of their makeshift carriage as tight as she could.

Duke took a deep breath and pushed the crank. After years spent unused, the rusty metal resisted. The chains in the winch shook as if stuck. But then something gave up the fight – or perhaps, more worryingly, came loose – and the wheel grunted counter-clockwise. After a tremendous, stomach-turning lurch, the pots began their slow journey up and down the shaft.

After a couple of rotations, Duke stopped.

"You sure you want to go through with this?" he called down to them.

"Nope," Ginger replied, shrugging, her forehead drenched in sweat. "But we're doing it anyway."

Duke turned the crank. Evans stood with his arms crossed, shaking his head. And Ginger and Ghost were slowly lowered into the belly of New Terra.

CHAPTER NINE

The giant pot scraped against the bottom of the shaft like a ship beaching against jagged rocks. There was no hinged door through which to disembark; Ginger and Ghost clambered over the lip of their iron carriage and threw themselves to the floor below.

Ginger rolled through the dirt, cursed under her breath, and watched as their pot stopped scraping the ground and began its rise back towards the surface. The thick chains rattled louder than ever. More fireflies flittered around the base of the mechanism, apparently unperturbed by the sudden noise.

The two women scrambled to their feet and scoured the cave for potential threats. The base of the mineshaft was wide, open and crudely cut into the foundations of the mountain; the walls were jagged and uneven, the floor not remotely level. Rotting beams propped up the precarious ceiling and thick swathes of rope-nets had done little to prevent rockslides. Wooden cart tracks were either nailed into the floor or left entirely loose, and many of the planks were missing. Small, dark tunnels with similarly derelict supports led further outwards and downwards in all directions.

No roaches, though.

Ginger went to shout back up the pit, then caught herself. Just because their makeshift elevator was making a lot of noise didn't mean her voice wouldn't bring a hive's worth of roaches running. They had to be smarter than that.

"Duke, do you read me?" She whispered into her headset. "We're at the bottom. You can stop turning the crank now."

The chains ceased moving as soon as she stopped talking. Duke's voice came through her comm unit a second later.

"Good to hear, boss. Everything clear down there?"

"Yeah. For now."

Ginger studied the base of the giant contraption. Once there might have been an elevated wooden platform for depositing carts of ore into the rotating containers, but now there was just a pile of bent nails and broken boards. Bad bloody luck, as per usual. To the left of the pot they'd hastily abandoned was another rusty winch system, a mirror image of the one up top.

"Good news. I'm looking at another crank. Get into the next pot and we'll move it from here."

"Sure. Thing is, Sergeant... Evans, he's—"

"You tell Evans to get his arse in that receptacle pronto or I'll ride back up and throw him down. And I don't want to hear any crap about 'keeping a lookout', got it? We're already behind schedule as it is."

"Yes, ma'am."

The chains shifted slightly as additional weight was added to the mechanism. A couple of pebbles tumbled down the side of the hole. Ginger wondered if it had sounded this rickety when *she* climbed in.

"We're in," Duke said after a long thirty seconds. "Evans, too."

"Glad to hear it. Hold tight. Bringing you down now."

Ginger grabbed the crank handle and pushed hard. It pushed back. She wasn't even half as strong as Duke, and unfortunately there wasn't enough of a grip for Ghost to make up the difference. But the aliens who lived on New Terra before them hadn't exactly been built like oxen, either. They were a short species with wide skulls and stubby hands. If they could operate machines like this, so could she.

The wheel slowly turned, grinding rust against rust. Tiny brown flecks spat out from the gears inside. The chain continued its reluctant cycle up and down the mountain. The pots groaned as they swung on their hooks.

And damn, was all of it noisy.

"God, I don't like this," said Ghost, scanning the tunnels with her submachine gun drawn. "I don't like this *at all.*"

"Keep focussed," Ginger groaned. "Not much further."

"Just hurry up, will you?" It wasn't like Ghost to get so anxious. "I think I hear something down here with us."

"So deal with it." Ginger was gritting her teeth so hard she feared they might crack. "What the hell's gotten into you?"

"Nothing," Ghost snapped back. She shook her head from side to side. "It's not usually just me against a whole nest, that's all."

Halfway. Ginger glanced up and, before she had to blink a bead of sweat out of her eye, she spotted Duke and Evans in one of the pots about halfway down the shaft, at best.

Dammit. Her hands were already starting to cramp and they still had most of the way to go.

Something crumbled on the other side of the cave.

"What was that?" Ghost snapped her gun from one tunnel to another. "Did *you* see that? Where it went?"

"Probably just the chains shaking some rocks loose. Who knows what damage all this mining did to the mountain."

"Bullshit, Ginger. Something's watching us and you know it."

"Hold it together, Private. You're supposed to be the hard-headed one in the fireteam, remember?"

"No, I'm supposed to be the goddamn *sniper!*"

Ginger somehow found the energy to push even harder. Either that, or the wheel was starting to come loose. She really hoped Ghost didn't get an itchy trigger finger. They wouldn't be able to get everybody out at once if they needed to make a quick escape. Somebody would have to stay behind to operate the crank.

Goddammit. Maybe Evans *should* have stayed up top after all.

"There it is again," said Ghost. "Don't tell me you didn't hear it this time."

Ginger would have frozen had turning the wheel not become an almost instinctive motion. There was no denying it – a scratchy, scrambling noise over by the wall to their right. Yet no matter how hard she stared, there was nothing to see but dark, inanimate rock.

"Keep close," she grunted. "Back up towards me, slowly."

Ghost did as instructed, keeping her eyes on the cavern's many nooks and crannies. Duke and Evans's pot was almost level with the cave roof now. In less than thirty seconds they'd be a full fireteam again. If there *was* something down there with them, they wouldn't face it alone.

A soft trickle of pebbles pattered against the top of Ghost's helmet. She sluggishly raised her head. Her eyes grew wide. Her jaw stiffened.

"Erm, Ginger? What… the hell… is that?"

Hanging from the ceiling was some sort of yellow centipede, about a dozen feet long and covered along its back by a hard, brown carapace. The pincers on the end of its innumerable legs looked hard enough to puncture rock. The mandibles to either side of the sphincter it called a mouth looked much worse.

The creature folded back on itself so that it dangled directly above Ghost's head, flared its appendages, and screamed.

"Move, Ghost!" Duke shouted, propping his rifle against the lip of his iron carriage and opening fire.

Ghost dived to the side just in time to avoid a streak of hot, green fluid spat from inside the centipede's mouth. The gunk sizzled against the stone. Lucky for her, the bug didn't get a second chance. It shrieked in fury as round after round from Duke's rifle – and a second later, Evans's too – peppered its armoured hide. Ginger simply stared for a moment, too shocked, or perhaps too exhausted, to truly register what was going on. Then she snapped out of her stupor, grabbed the rifle off her back and joined in the shooting as well.

The shell on its back must have been grown of thicker stuff than those on its roach counterparts, because most of Sigma's shots barely cracked the surface. They sure got its attention, though. It swung its upper half back up again, took aim at the pot still six or seven metres above the ground, and spat out another acidic jet.

Duke and Evans ducked as the liquid splashed against the side of their cover. The metal hissed, but the iron was much too thick for any real damage to be done. A tiny globule spilled over the top and splashed Duke on the sleeve, however. He kicked backwards in a mad panic and hurriedly wiped it off against the pot's interior before it could burn through to his skin.

In aiming at the pot, the centipede exposed more of its fleshy yellow underbelly. Ginger exhaled as calmly as she could and fired a quick burst before it could swing back and take another shot at Ghost. One of its spindly legs burst off at the joint. Another round punctured what looked to be its midriff, though God only knew where the ugly, wormy thing kept its internal organs.

Ghost had rolled out of the way and now staggered to her feet. She sprayed about a dozen rounds at the bug only seconds after Ginger took her own handful of shots, but it was enough time for the centipede to pin itself against the roof of the cave again. Another leg popped free with a shower of blood and pus; the rest of Ghost's rounds clattered ineffectively against its scarred carapace.

Duke and Evans opened fire again, taking care not to touch the outside of their pot. The centipede let out a pair of short, sharp screeches and then scuttled across the cave ceiling towards one of the tunnels at the far end. Sigma's gunshots dripped to an echoey stop.

"Everyone in one piece?" Ginger called out, not lowering her rifle from where she saw the bug leave.

"Yeah, yeah, we're good," Evans barked down at her. "Just get us the hell out of this thing."

Ginger rushed back to the crank and lowered it enough that they could jump down without twisting their ankles. They chose to hop over the left side of the pot rather than risk touching where the centipede's spittle had stained the iron a chalky white colour. With her arms as weak as boiled spaghetti, Ginger gathered her shaken fireteam together.

"It won't get any easier from here on out," she said, checking her rifle's magazine. "From now on, we stick together. Cover each other's backs."

"I'm surprised our shots didn't attract more bugs," said Ghost, catching her breath. "Maybe this nest is already dead."

"Did you forget all those flying roaches outside?" said Evans.

"Well, maybe they're the only bugs left," Duke suggested. "Besides our new thirty-legged friend, obviously."

"Doesn't matter." Ginger slammed the magazine back into her rifle. "The deeper we go, the more likely we'll find one of those cocoons Command wants. Let's get a move on."

They crossed the cave, each of them covering a different quarter in case the centipede made a second attempt to dissolve them. One good thing had come from their skirmish with the creepy crawly, at least. Wounded, the bug would most likely retreat back towards the safety of the hive's main chamber. With any luck, the same tunnel would take Sigma where they needed to go, too.

Whether that was to their objective, or a short, violent death, was another matter altogether.

The ceiling of the tunnel was lower on account of the old species' smaller stature, but the tunnel was better dug than the caves as well. Smashed lanterns hung from ropes looping along the walls. Every stone surface was either smoothly cut or supported by girders of iron, not the rotting wood seen elsewhere in the subterranean system. A good thing, too – trickles of freshwater ran out from some of the cracks. An underground stream. Even bugs needed to drink in order to survive, Ginger supposed.

More fireflies lit their way. None of the squad used flashlights. It was still too dark to see properly, but bugs or no bugs, they couldn't risk attracting any more attention.

Ghost nudged Evans in the ribs.

"You ever gone down into a nest before, newbie?" she whispered.

"No," he bitterly replied. "They always this quiet?"

"Sometimes. Sometimes not. Depends whether the roaches are preoccupied with anything else. There's been some real horror shows, apparently. Whole companies torn to pieces 'cause they strolled right into a full house."

"Thanks, mate. That's really helped put my nerves to rest."

"Don't sweat it," Duke whispered conspiratorially. "The first nest we busted was under Rhinegarde. All the roaches were busy fighting the marines fleeing the city. By the time they caught onto us, we'd already dropped a sack of C-4 on their arses. And you know what? This nest seems even quieter."

"Quieter than you lot, at any rate," Ginger grunted.

"We'll be in and out in no time," Duke added, slapping a weary Evans on the back.

The tunnel continued straight ahead, unlike those of "natural" bug nests, which tended to spiral inwards and downwards with only a modest angle of descent. It had almost certainly been dug by hand – stubby alien hand, too. It must have taken them years. Decades, even. Every now and then they passed a workstation, be it a rickety desk for laying tools or a bench on which the exhausted miners could rest.

"Whatever they were digging for," said Duke. "D'ya reckon they found it?"

"They sure found a lot of ore, if that's what you mean," Ghost whispered.

"Shut up," Ginger snapped. "All of you. There's a light up ahead and I don't think it's more goddamn fireflies."

Everyone snapped their mouths shut and their rifles up. The end of their tunnel emitted a warm, orange glow, too large and consistent to be the harmless critters – not unless a few dozen of them had swarmed together in some sort of luminescent orgy, at least. And she doubted any of the old race's lanterns were still burning after all this time.

Christ. When a random underground fire feels like the best option you can hope for, that's when you know you're in trouble.

Ginger couldn't hear anything. No scuttling, no scratching. No rocks crumbling, no water dripping. Just the sinister silence of a few million tonnes of mountain lurking right above their heads.

She nodded to the others, who nodded back. They stepped into the glowing cave beyond.

"Sweet Mary and Joseph," Duke whispered, breaking into a smile. "Ladies and gentlemen, I think we're in luck."

It took everything Ginger had not to laugh in relief. It wasn't a cave so much as a loading station where ore could be chucked onto carts to be brought topside. Enormous, naturally occurring caverns of darkness lay beyond. And lining the floor were two rows of three fleshy cocoons, each chrysalis the size of a small car and softly glowing from within.

"Abandoned?" Ghost peered over the edge of the platform and admired the vast drop. Her voice carried. "Or purposely kept out of the way, do you think?"

"Who cares?" said Evans, handing Duke his knife. "Let's cut out a sample and then get the hell out of this place."

"Why am I cutting it?" Duke replied with suspicion. "I'm the one with the receptacle, remember."

"Suit yourself," Evans said with a shrug.

He gently tossed the knife in his hand, caught it by the handle, and crouched down beside the nearest cocoon. After cautiously prodding its gelatinous shell with the flat of the blade, he plunged the knife into the middle of the blob and started forcefully cutting down its length.

"How big a piece do you want?" he asked, smirking up at Duke.

"Just shut up and stick *something* in there," the big guy replied, holding out the open flask for him.

Evans cut out a rough cube of, well, whatever it was a bug cocoon was made of, and let it slide off his blade into the receptacle. Duke secured the lid and then returned the container to its place amongst the rest of his inventory. When Evans went to stand up again, Ginger put a hard hand on his shoulder.

"Not so fast," she said, eyeing the chrysalis. "I want to see what's actually inside one of these things."

"Really?" Evans sighed.

"Aren't you curious?" Ginger raised an eyebrow. "It's not like Command'll tell us anything they find."

"Fine. Whatever." Evans shook his head. "But after this I'm outta here, whether the rest of you suicidal halfwits are with me or not."

He stabbed his knife back into the cocoon and sliced it from head to toe as if he were unzipping a bodybag. With a grimace – not to mention Duke's rifle primed and ready in case something eight-legged came bursting out – he prised the two halves open. Everyone staggered backwards when they saw what lay inside.

"Christ Almighty," Ghost gasped. "No wonder the boffins upstairs want a sample so bad."

It turned out unzipping a bodybag wasn't far off the mark. Beneath the thick, translucent crust was a cavity filled with gloopy, radiant fluid. Submerged inside that, a body. But not a roach body. Not even that of a human.

It was a corpse from the race that came before.

"I didn't think there were any of these guys left," said Ginger, unable to stop staring at it. "Skeletons, sure. But nothing, you know, intact. This is incredible."

"Intact's a bit of a stretch," said Ghost, pulling a face. "I pity the poor freaks if they're *supposed* to look like that."

At least one aspect of the alien's physiology was recognisable from the statues erected around their derelict cities – its wide, rugby-ball shaped head. Whoever this creature had once been, its eyes were closed, but it didn't look as if it were dead.

It looked as if it were put under with anaesthetic.

An inflexible organic tube ran out from the side of the crust and down the alien's throat, and spread across the outside of its mouth like some sort of breathing mask. One of its hands had lost all definition, its stubby fingers having fused together into a hard, boney stump. Both of its legs were far larger and more muscular than any of the skeletons the UEC had previously found suggested, and completely disproportionate to the rest of its body. Random patches of dark brown chitin had sprouted across its bloated torso. And even its skull was starting to change shape, to squash inwards and grow callouses. Some form of metamorphosis was clearly taking place.

"My God," said Evans, turning to stare at the rest of them. "It's turning into one of those things, ain't it?"

"A mutant bug," Ginger replied numbly. "Yeah. Jesus, I think he's right."

"We've got to take it with us," said Duke, suddenly growing alert. "Command's gonna want to see this."

"How, exactly?" Ginger shook her head. "I don't know if this thing's technically alive or dead, but it sure won't be breathing if we cut off its life support."

"So?" Duke squatted down and started to film it with the camera built into his helmet. "Even dead, it's still the find of a century."

Ghost indicated to the receptacle hanging from Duke's hip.

"Yeah, I'm with Duke," she said, whistling. "After seeing this, I don't think a sample's gonna cut it."

"Erm, guys?" Evans snapped his trembling rifle back up in the direction of the tunnel behind them. "If we don't do something sharpish, I'm not sure *any* of us are getting back out alive."

Ginger spun around with her own rifle raised. She counted six garden-variety roaches scuttling down the tunnel walls towards them. Thank God they weren't flamers. Faint, impatient screeches told her more of their kind were on the way behind.

"Stay calm," she said. "Remember – they're the ones in the bottleneck, not us."

"Yeah," Ghost said hesitantly. "So why aren't they moving?"

Despite the roaches' bloodthirsty enthusiasm, none of them came further than the end of the tunnel. They gathered inside the opening, fiercely clambering over one another, snapping their mandibles with rage... but not so much as a spindly antennae crossed the threshold.

"Don't tell me they're scared of this place," said Duke.

"Somehow," Ghost replied, "I don't think it's that."

A dark shape swept up from the cavern, so large that it seemed to distort the very air around them. It latched onto the edge of the metal platform with a thunderous crash. The whole mountain seemed to quake.

Slowly, Sigma turned to face it.

Their eyes went up, and up, and up.

"Oh shit," Ginger whispered. "I think we found the queen."

CHAPTER TEN

The queen latched onto the side of the mining platform with a pair of giant bristly claws. Others, further down her body, dug into the stone walls like climbing hooks. The whole cavern shook with her weight.

She dwarfed even the largest units amongst her roach army. Ginger reckoned she was easily twice the size of a tank bug, maybe even double one of those flying bombers. It was hard to put things in perspective, really, what with a single insect occupying every inch of her vision.

The queen's body consisted of three segments like a wasp – a head, abdomen and thorax – with similar proportions for each. Her abdomen hung far below the edge of the platform. Glancing down, Ginger spotted no stinger. Instead, she suspected the bulbous mass hanging beneath her housed dozens, maybe hundreds of roach eggs – they were the breed of bug the queen herself most resembled, after all.

The thorax – that is, the insect's midriff – was almost entirely protected by a shell of off-white chitin armour. And not just that. Patches of the same purple and yellow gunk they'd seen plastered across the factory doors reinforced her particularly vulnerable spots, too. Man, they'd thought the tank bugs were tough to kill. Compared to this monster, they were nothing but woodlice under a hardback book.

And then came the head. Christ almighty, the head. A pair of serrated mandibles the size of drop ship wings flanked a series of vertical slits through which smaller bugs scuttled in and out. Food carriers, Ginger guessed. Unlike the roaches, however, which only had the two eyes – small and forward facing, more like those of an apex predator than the compound eyes of a normal insect – the queen boasted a whopping six pairs, starting largest at the front and running in twin curves towards the back of her head which, of course, was as armour-plated as her middle.

"Sod it," Evans spluttered, raising his rifle. "If I'm dying down here, I'm taking that bitch with me."

"Hold your fire." Ginger smacked his gun back down. "The roaches aren't coming any further. I want to know why."

"You sure they just don't want to infringe on their boss's feeding time?" Ghost said, frantically switching her aim from one target to the other.

"Yeah, I'm with Ghost." Duke looked as if he'd stepped out of a shower, he was sweating so hard. "Queenie thinks we're a goddamn snack."

"Maybe." Ginger tried to keep from trembling. "But then, why hasn't she eaten us yet? And if *she* hasn't," she added, quickly glancing at the impatient roaches behind them, "why haven't they?"

Because I will not let them.

Ginger dropped to her knees and clutched at her head. It felt like it was swelling inside her helmet... like her brain was a bowl of popcorn turning in a microwave oven. The rest of her fireteam collapsed in much the same way. She guessed she didn't need to ask them whether they'd heard the voice, too.

"Heard" wasn't quite right, though. "Heard" implied sound waves and ears. This voice had spoken from directly inside her head, louder than even her own internal monologue.

As the pain subsided, Ginger squinted up at the royal roach.

"Was that you?"

You hear me.

Another flash of pain. This time was slightly less agonising than the first. Evans swore loudly, but luckily he'd dropped his rifle. Ginger gritted her teeth in anticipation of the next answer.

"How?"

Because I choose it. My children are scattered across this world-hive and beyond. I hear them, and them me. When I command, they follow. One brood. One eternal voice carried through the silence. And now I turn that voice to you.

"But we don't speak bug, goddammit." Ghost pushed herself up onto her feet. "We speak English."

The queen shifted her colossal mass and blinked her dozen eyes at them heavily.

How you designate your crude vocalisations is of no concern. My children hear you, and I them. A hundred-thousand voices in as many tongues, scattered across the world-hive. We did not recognise your words. But we listened. First to the Essyen, and then to you. A million minds working as one. Yours is a simple language of one sense alone. No vibrations, no pheromones, no data shared through taste. Only sounds. I speak your simple words through our complex ways. We would not expect a brood as young as your own to understand.

"The Essyen?" Ginger stood up straight; the words were getting easier now. "You mean the people who lived on this planet before?"

Before. You do not comprehend before – were not there before. The Essyen were but simple burrow-dwellers when we first came here. Our brood's evolution far surpassed their own. This world-hive belonged to us from the beginning. We ARE the beginning. We ARE before.

"Makes no sense." Duke wiped a small trickle of blood away from under his nose with the back of his hand. "The race who lived on this world before us had cities, societies, culture. You only killed them all off a few years back. Doesn't sound like the beginning to me."

"What we doing, Sarge?" Evans whispered to Ginger. He picked up his rifle. "We should be killing these freaks while we still can. This ain't right."

"Gotta agree with Evans," Ghost hissed out the corner of her mouth. "We need an exit strategy, now."

Colonisation occurred four and a quarter solar cycles ago. The queen flexed her mandibles as she answered Duke. *We came ten thousand cycles earlier. Our brood-sac tore through the cold and empty darkness for millennia, searching for a new world-hive. Here it crashed, and here our eggs lay in wait. Ready to hatch. Ready to breed.*

"Here?" Duke pointed a nervous finger at the platform beneath his feet. "Are you saying you came here on a comet? That this mountain is where it struck?"

Ginger stared past the queen into the hollow caverns beyond as comprehension dawned.

"You must have been trapped down here under all the rock and ice," she said. "Your hibernation would have probably never ended had the Essyen not started mining. I guess they were after the comet's rare minerals. Jesus. That's some damn bad luck."

For them.

"Possible exit," Ghost whispered with her back turned to the queen. "Three o'clock."

Ginger didn't acknowledge Private Flores, nor even look in the direction she was suggesting. If Ghost said she'd found a way out, Ginger trusted her. Out the corner of her eye, she spotted Duke switching one rifle attachment out for another. Good. When the time came, they needed to move fast.

"So what's your plan now?" she asked the giant bug. "We're more advanced than the Essyen. Surely you know this war's almost over."

The hairs across the queen's body bristled. The roaches in the tunnel behind them snapped and screeched. Two millipedes of similar breed to the one they fought earlier crept out from tunnels in the rock walls to either side of the platform, scuttled down the queen's frontmost legs, and wrapped around her narrow neck.

Your brood came from the stars also, she replied. *You fight hard. But it matters not. We are legion. There will always be more.*

"Not if we kill the bitch laying the eggs," Evans spat, raising his rifle again. "Screw the rest of you. I know my orders."

"Stand down, Private!" Ginger glared at him. "In case you forgot, our orders are to get the sample topside. Follow my lead, goddammit."

She turned back to the queen.

"The more roaches you breed, the more of those unholy mutants you build, the more of your brood we'll kill. Or you could surrender. You're clearly intelligent. I'm sure our two hive-minds could arrive at some sort of compromise."

"Are you seriously trying to broker a peace treaty with the bugs?" Evans spat through gritted teeth. His eyes looked ready to pop out of his skull. "Are you out of your bloody mind?"

"I'm trying to get us out of here alive, you idiot."

Ghost pulled Evans away. Ginger tightened her grip on her rifle.

"We've got entire battalions of troops above ground," she shouted. "More than enough to wipe out you and your remaining babies. There can't be that many of you left, right? Let us go, or they'll storm this place and kill you. Be smart. This is a big planet. We can figure something out."

The queen turned her massive head upwards. Listening, perhaps. Ginger's stomach tightened. Was the leader of the bug army actually considering her offer?

Your numbers are considerable, yes. And you brought some of your best soldiers from all across the world-hive. We listened to the wireless voices with which you fill the air. You think this is our brood's final stand.

The queen bowed her head and fixed Sigma with her dozen black eyes.

It is yours.

"This whole mission's a trap." Ginger swallowed hard as she realised the queen's intentions. "They've drawn us into a goddamn kill-box."

There is nowhere for you humans to run. You stand between the ocean and the endless frost. You are surrounded, but you were right. We ARE smart. And our brood is nothing if not patient. Yours, however...

"Get Staff Sergeant Baker on the line," Ginger snapped at Duke. "Tell him to get everyone away from the factory."

"Comms are down," Duke replied, shaking his head. "No signal. We must be too far below ground."

The roaches occupying the tunnel behind them grew restless, snapping and screeching and thrashing at the wooden supports holding up the walls. The queen kept them at bay with a flick of her tree-trunk antennae.

It is almost time. We had not spoken directly to your brood before. It has proven... enlightening. Your kind will be harvested and your learnings regarding star-travel added to our own. But my children grow hungry. This conversation has reached its end.

"You bet it has," Ginger shouted as she turned to her fireteam. "Now!"

Duke turned his rifle upwards. During their conversation with the bug queen, he'd swapped out the shotgun attachment on its undercarriage for a single-use grenade launcher. He pulled the trigger and a small canister shot out with a short *thum* sound. The queen roared as it detonated against her carapace-covered face and showered her with rock from the cavern ceiling.

Ginger and Ghost spun around and emptied their clips at the throng of roaches suddenly pouring through the tunnel behind them. Either Evans caught on quicker than Ginger gave him credit or he was simply swept up in the moment, because he joined the firefight also.

"Stairwell over by the east wall," Ghost shouted above the thunder of their rifles. "Must be how the aliens who built this place got up and down."

"Well, we ain't going back the way we came," Evans replied. The tunnel was a strobe-lit bottleneck of bug parts and blood.

The queen turned and climbed down from the rock, her armoured head slightly charred but otherwise undamaged by Duke's grenade. As she lumbered back into the caverns,

Ginger spotted thousands more bugs scuttling across the subterranean walls in their direction.

The queen was right. They *were* legion.

"Jesus Christ," Duke gasped. "I don't fancy our chances much that way, either."

"Stairs it is," said Ginger. She could taste iron. "Let's just hope there hasn't been a cave-in. Everybody, move!"

They sprinted towards the square of darkness chiseled into the mountain wall. As their aim lost its accuracy and their assault on the tunnel faltered, furious roaches spilled out onto the metal platform. It didn't take long for the bugs to start sprinting towards the stairwell, too.

"Got anything else in that bag of tricks of yours?" Ginger shouted to Duke, firing semi-controlled bursts behind her. "More grenades? A goddamn proximity mine?"

"I wish." Duke let one magazine drop from his rifle and then slammed in another. "That was my last explosive. I'm out."

Ginger's heart fell. As they neared the opening, the stairs crept into view. They were wooden. Even if only a few years old – this deep into the mines, they could have succumbed to rot.

She hated to admit it even to herself, but the bug queen may have been right.

It looked like their time was up.

CHAPTER ELEVEN

They raced up the rickety wooden steps. Some sagged beneath their boots; others had snapped off in the years since construction began. The whole towering structure quaked and swayed as they climbed it.

"What's the plan, Sarge?" Evans screamed.

"What the hell do you think it is?" Ginger screamed back at him. "We go up!"

The stairwell doubled back on itself over and over like an old New York fire escape. It was hard to tell how high the hollow shaft of stone actually went. A hundred metres or more, surely. The only light cast upon its steps was from the same tiny fireflies fluttering around the rest of the facility, and it wasn't as if their destination up top was any brighter than the caverns below.

Speaking of which…

"We've got company," Duke grunted, pausing only briefly to glance down through the gaps between steps.

"So we do," Ginger wheezed in exasperation, peering over the side of the precarious scaffolding. "Just keep climbing. Don't look down!"

Easier said than done. Even Ginger had a hard time tearing her eyes from the hole in the mountain wall. Scores of roaches crawled over one another – *snapped* at one another – as they spilled through from the mining platform on the other side. A few had clocked where their fleeing prey were headed and were already scuttling up the rocky walls towards them.

"Are you absolutely sure you don't have another grenade on you somewhere?" Ghost gasped as she ran up the steps beside Duke. "C-4? Phosphorus? Hell, even a goddamn claymore?"

"I told you," he coughed. "I'm all out."

"No explosives," Ginger shouted, pulling Evans up the stairs behind them. "You go setting something off and this whole damn stairwell comes crashing down. Firearms only."

"Yeah," Evans spluttered, "as if *that's* gonna do a whole lotta good."

"Keep your head, Private." Ginger shoved him forward. "We've survived worse than this."

"You might have. But I haven't!"

They kept climbing. The sound of roaches chittering and screeching and scratching kept growing louder. Ginger's lungs felt as coarse as the striking strip on the side of a matchbox. About as hot, too. Her thighs were as stiff as tyre irons. But still her fireteam soldiered on, grabbing the wooden railings as they rounded each corner. Swinging themselves up the next flight of steps. Jumping over the few that were missing.

Bug trap or not, they weren't ready to die just yet.

"Look sharp," said Ghost, raising her submachine gun. "Here they come!"

The first of the roaches scuttled across the rock beside

them. It flared its mandibles as it screamed. Duke spun around and blew its head open with a blast from his rifle's shotgun attachment. Blood splattered across the walkway. The decapitated bug flailed back down the shaft past its endless brethren.

Ginger glanced up again.

Still too far to go.

But they weren't *completely* out of options.

"Half a dozen flights above us," she gasped as she resumed sprinting up the steps. "See it?"

"Kinda busy looking down, if I'm honest," Duke grunted, blasting a second bug as it drew level with him.

Ghost sprayed rounds into another roach climbing up on the other side, then followed Ginger's eye-line.

"Some sort of pulley lift, right?" She leaned over the side of the railing and emptied half of her clip into the swarm below. "So?"

"If it can ferry tools down to the mine, maybe it can carry us back up to the surface," said Ginger. "Probably a lot quicker than we can walk, too."

"That old thing?" Evans fired his rifle at one roach after another so fast, he didn't even have time to check his kills. "Seriously? It looks like it'll collapse the second we set foot on it."

"So did the stairs," said Duke, shrugging. "Worth a shot."

"You're insane! What if it just sends us crashing back down?"

"I'll send you crashing back down if you don't shut the hell up," Ginger muttered under her breath.

"*What?*"

"I said get on the damn platform! That's an order!"

A bug climbed up the outside of the staircase and dropped onto the short landing in front of Ginger. She fired from the hip without stopping, puncturing the roach with close to twenty rounds and leaving it a bloody, twitching heap on the splintered planks, then continued heading upwards. The platform was now only a couple of flights away.

She tried not to look at the walls too much. It was hard to tell which parts of them were formed of slimy rock and which were crawling with slobbering insects. Sigma couldn't kill all of them. Maybe even the entire battalion couldn't. Their only hope was getting out – out of the shaft, out of the tundra, out of the whole goddamn operation.

Even if they did make it back outside, would Command listen to them and evacuate? Or would it already be too late?

A roach reached the pulley lift at the same time Ginger did, catching her off-guard. A shot was fired close to Ginger's ear, rendering her momentarily deaf. Duke had fired off a round from his handgun – Ginger assumed his rifle was empty – and knocked the bug off the platform with a neat headshot.

"Everybody on," Ginger shouted. "Go!"

Duke climbed up onto the stairwell railing and jumped the two foot gap to the platform. It visibly shifted a couple of inches under his weight. Ghost followed with slightly less impact, though there was no ignoring the ominous creaking sound as the strained ropes pulled at the planks in each corner.

"You next," Ginger said to Evans, while Duke and Ghost fired past them at the encroaching roaches.

Evans hesitated, scrunched up his face, then huffed.

"Sod it."

He leapt across. Ginger didn't even wait for him to reach safety before doing the same. She could almost feel the bugs' pincers snapping inches from her neck.

She heard something crack as she landed. One of the wooden beams on top of the platform, hopefully, rather than anything offering support beneath it. She didn't much care what the pulley was left looking like once they were done using it, just so long as it survived the trip.

Ghost peered back down the shaft.

"Ginger..."

Roaches flowed up every inch of the tunnel as if they were water gushing up a pipe. They climbed the brittle walls; they scaled the wooden staircase. With any luck the damn rotten thing would collapse under the weight of them all.

But luck was in pretty short supply this mission.

"How the hell does this thing work?" Ginger grunted and pulled at the ropes holding it above the abyss. The platform stayed where it was. Maybe it even dropped slightly.

Evans turned to look at her with a pair of white, saucer-shaped eyes.

"You're asking us that *now?*"

Everyone emptied their magazines at the approaching tide of bugs. There was no stopping them. For every roach that fell from the walls, another two took its place. One tried leaping across from the stairs opposite; Duke blasted it back the way it came.

"Up there," said Ghost. "Counterweight."

Ginger stared up the mineshaft. Hanging almost directly above them was a giant, cylindrical slab of stone. It too hung from a fraying rope, presumably the same as theirs and looping around a winch in the ceiling they couldn't yet see. Some sort of brake mechanism kept it latched in position.

"If that goes down, we go up," she said. "The question is, how do we get it to move from here?"

"I don't think the engineers designed it with this exact

scenario in mind," Duke grunted, switching back to his regular semi-automatic ammo. "Probably a lever up top, or something."

"We don't have time to talk about this!" Evan released one magazine and slammed in another. "Hurry up and bloody *do* something!"

Another roach jumped at the platform, took a chunk out of one of the planks with a flailing claw, and then disappeared into the darkness.

"Screw it." Ghost grabbed her sniper rifle off her back and squinted through its scope. "Here goes nothing."

"Wait!" Ginger held up her hand. "Don't—"

Ghost took the shot. The resulting boom was twice as deafening as Duke's pistol, or even the whole fireteam's rifles being fired together at such close range. But Ginger didn't have time to complain about the fresh bout of ringing in her ears. Ghost's round pierced the braking mechanism and the counterweight came barrelling down the shaft. Within seconds, their platform was going in the opposite direction.

Going quite a bit quicker than she'd anticipated, too.

She fell onto her backside and grabbed one of the ropes attached to the corners of their platform. Ghost pinwheeled backwards with her rifle swinging off her arm by only its strap. She probably would have gone right over the edge had Duke not grabbed her in a rather undignified manner by her bulletproof chest plate. Evans, remarkably, remained upright.

The rocks to all sides became a dark grey blur. She could hear a whistling noise growing higher in pitch as they ascended. The rope whipping through the winch, maybe? Or burning and fraying, seconds away from snapping, ready to send the platform tumbling back down the shaft like the counterweight before it...

The four of them gathered their balance enough to collect together in the middle of the lift. They glanced up as the shaft raced by. There didn't appear to be a great deal of it left.

"Oh crap," said Ghost. "Is that the roof coming towards us?"

They were thirty metres away, maybe fewer. Ginger could see the winch through which the rope was whistling. It was shaking about like crazy, tearing itself from the metal struts.

"What happens when we reach it?" Evans shouted. "Do we stop? Please tell me we're going to stop!"

"One way or another," Ginger replied. She gulped. "But something tells me we shouldn't wait for the pulley to do it for us. On my word, we jump."

"*Where?*"

"Anywhere that isn't up, goddamnit!"

"What, like *down?*"

"Now!"

They leapt from the platform when it was only metres from the winch; the boards smashed into pieces against the iron girders in the ceiling above. An almighty boom rose up from the bottom of the shaft as the counterweight crashed to the floor below.

Ginger's hunch had been right. The top of the hole was surrounded on all sides by a dusty cart delivery room. She and Duke had jumped towards the side closest to the pulley-lift and crashed onto the metal floor. Ghost and Evans, on the other hand, chose the side opposite. Though they would have fallen short of the hole's actual perimeter, they landed on the very precipice of the wooden stairwell adjacent to their makeshift elevator. It creaked, some of the planks broke... but luckily for them both, it was secured to the surrounding delivery room with a row of bolts each as big as Ginger's fist.

She sat up and groaned through gritted teeth. Duke rose to his feet, staggered towards the hole and then back again, and then leaned forwards with his hand pressed against the wall.

"I'm never taking a lift again," he grumbled. "Or the stairs. I'm sticking to the ground floor for the rest of my life."

"That might not be very long," Ghost wheezed, peering down over the rickety stairs. "They're still coming. We need to move, maybe lose them in the factory."

"I just want to get out of this place," said Ginger, spitting a globule of blood onto the floor. "Hell, I just want to get off this whole damn planet."

"Yeah?" Duke pulled Ginger to her feet while Ghost and Evans limped around the hole to meet them. "I reckon our friends coming up the mineshaft wouldn't mind that, too."

They hobbled past the abandoned carts, the boxes of mining tools and the piles of unrefined ore. There were no windows, so either the shaft was located within a room inside another room, or the species who occupied New Terra before them hadn't been too fussed about their workers' health. Probably not a pressing concern, Ginger supposed, for people about to head down into a mine. But it meant she had no way of telling where in the godforsaken foundry they were now. The ground floor, like Duke said? Probably. But were they around the corner from the gunky front doors, or still buried somewhere deep underneath the mountain?

All they could do was follow the cart tracks and hope they led somewhere safe. Or safer, at least.

There was only one exit to the room – a long, narrow corridor filled with junk from the Essyen's panicked evacuation. Hardly ideal with a swarm of roaches coming after them. Even worse if another group of bugs came rushing down the other side.

Beggars can't be choosers, though.

They sprinted down its length, the cuts and bruises from their crash-landing ignored or forgotten, spending as much of that time staring back down the way they came as they did the path forward. Ginger supposed they were lucky the facility had been left largely empty above ground. Had the bug queen not permitted them entry into the caverns in order to quench her alien curiosity, the whole place might have been crawling with insects already.

A screech from behind caught Ginger by surprise. She spun around to discover a roach down at the other end of the corridor, standing up on its powerful hind legs as if challenging her to a fight. Ginger froze, suddenly reminded of her first encounter with a bug back in the forest. It had been like an insectoid werewolf in the moonlight. They were towering, formidable opponents, one on one.

And now half a dozen more roaches scuttled past it, snapping their mandibles at her, at each other, at the bric-a-brac piled up in the way.

"Run," she grunted. "Doesn't matter where, just run!"

They followed the single track to the end of the corridor. It didn't break off into splinter tracks; it didn't deviate. Ginger hoped it would lead them back to the central cart interchange they'd seen at the front of the factory. When they barged into the larger tool repository full of bare shelves on the other side, they were met with two more open doorways. Duke, leading the group, chose the one through which the cart rails continued. The tracks had to be leading *somewhere*.

No sooner had they reached the next corridor than the roaches poured in from the one behind. Sigma let loose at the bugs, splattering the metal walls with blood, filling the corridor with ricochets, piling up the bodies in a bid to slow the horde down.

If only for a few short moments.

They turned to run down the next corridor. Quite literally down, it turned out – the corridor sloped at a steep angle towards the storey below. The cart tracks had other plans, apparently, disappearing into a small, dark tunnel to the left of the entrance before the descent could properly start.

"For Christ's sake," Duke groaned. "Do we seriously have to go back down *again?*"

"You really want to go back and find a different route?" Ghost snapped at him. "Just go!"

They raced down the ramp in near-total darkness; only a pair of fireflies lit their way, and their view of their destination was blocked by the ceiling sloping above them. Evans turned and fired as the first roach breached the opening at the top of the ramp. The rapid muzzle flash cast their movements in stark stop-motion. Ginger did the same, stepping backwards almost as quickly as she could pull her rifle's trigger, as more bugs clambered over the roach's corpse.

"It's the main lobby," Ghost shouted excitedly. "I think I can hear the drills outside!"

Ginger glanced over her shoulder while trying to keep the endless wave of roaches at bay. As far as she was concerned, each part of the foundry looked identical to the rest – a mix of copper sheets, iron girders and lots and lots of stone, covered liberally by a sheet of dust. That the hall at the bottom of the ramp was littered with discarded mine carts and draped with loops of chain hardly confirmed anything. But Ghost was right – even over all the gunfire, she *could* hear the sound of the UEC's drills trying to break through. They must have been getting close.

But close wasn't close enough. They needed a way out *now*.

"Doors," Duke huffed. "End of the ramp. Gotta close 'em."

Ginger was almost through the doors in question by the time she actually noticed them. Big bronze things to either side of the ramp's end, each a good six inches thick. They were standing wide open. Pale quarter-circle grooves were cut into the floor where they'd been repeatedly dragged open and shut.

"Two on each door," Ginger gasped. "Get them closed!"

Ghost and Duke grabbed the door to the left the second they were through the sloping corridor, Ginger and Evans the door to the right. Everyone shoved as hard as they could. The scraping sound of the doors as they ground against the stone floor almost drowned out the rumble of the roaches. Almost.

They got them shut just as the first bugs slammed into the other side. The doors threatened to smash open again, but Duke bravely pressed his back against them while Ghost found an iron bar to slot through their handles. Ginger and Evans grabbed one of the empty carts nearby and used it to form a barricade, just for good measure.

The bugs screamed and slashed at the doors, which continued to buckle and creak.

"Reckon it'll hold?" asked Ghost.

Ginger shook her head.

"No, but it'll buy us some time."

Evans backed away from the rest of them, shaking his head.

"Buy us some time for what?" he spluttered. "You heard that bitch down there. We're already as good as—"

Evans went rigid and his chest hitched forwards. A long, hooked stinger burst through his mouth, shattering his teeth and casting his wide, bloodshot eyes to the heavens. Evans let out a gurgling whine, then collapsed to the floor as the stinger whipped back out again.

A winged, scorpion-like creature scuttled across the ceiling above the spot where Evans had stood. It hissed at them by shaking its elongated tail like a rattlesnake. Duke replied by blasting it at almost point-blank range with his shotgun attachment. The bug collapsed beside Evans – *after* showering him with half a dozen body parts.

"Oh, Jesus." Ghost stared at the private. "Is he...?"

"Dead? Yeah." Ginger carefully turned Private Evans over. The bug had punched a hole right through the back of his neck. "We should have been more careful. We should have secured the hall first."

"Then we never would have got those doors closed and we'd all be dead," said Duke, resting his hand on her shoulder. "Wasn't your fault, Ginger. No way you could have—ah, *shit!*"

Duke winced and dropped to one knee as a second stinger-bug swept through the air behind him, slashing the back of his leg with its barbed tail before disappearing down one of the hall's other corridors.

"Are you okay, Duke?" Ghost asked. "How bad is it?"

"Never mind me," Duke grunted, waving at the escaping bug. "Damn thing took the sample!"

Ginger inspected Duke's leg. He was right – it hadn't been going in for the kill. His fatigues were torn but the wound, though certain to scar, was superficial. The clip securing the sample to his belt had been the bug's target. Evans's death must have been a distraction.

The hive-mind at work, Ginger guessed. No doubt the queen was behind this attack. Then again, the queen was behind *all* the attacks – a quite literal central intelligence.

Ghost grabbed her submachine gun and fired at the bugs buzzing down the corridor. She seemed more concerned with getting revenge for Duke than retrieving the sample. For all they knew, her rounds had just blown the canister to pieces. She succeeded in hitting one of the critters, at least – blood splashed against the wall of the corridor, even if it didn't stop the ugly bastard in question from flying.

"You okay to move?" Ginger asked.

"Yeah, think so." Duke winced as he rose to his feet. "Just need to walk it off, s'all. Fingers crossed it ain't venomous…"

"Well, you won't have long to find out." Ghost nodded at the front doors. "We'll get you checked over by a medic, pronto."

The drills were almost through. The weird, hardened residue that once seemed so immovable was now cracked and crumbling apart.

"No way." Duke shook his head. "It's like what Ginger said last time we were here. We ain't leaving without that sample. We ain't going back to Command empty-handed."

"You can barely stand," Ghost replied. "At this rate you won't be going back at all."

"Bollocks. I'm fine. We can all go lie down in the med bay together when the job's done."

Ginger looked to the barricade behind them, still shaking from the horde of roaches, then to the doors so soon to be drilled open by the UEC outside, and then finally to the dark corridor down which the flying critters had fled.

She sighed. They were almost out, and yet it seemed they were no closer to being finished than when they started.

"Duke's right. I hate it, but it's true. That cocoon sample is clearly of the utmost importance to the UEC. Something to do with the queen or recoding genetic material, I bet. Doesn't matter. They want it – that's the objective. That said, we need to get outside and prepare everyone for what's coming. If they're still drilling, my guess is they don't know yet. So let's hustle, all right?"

Ghost smirked determinedly.

"Yes, ma'am."

Ginger bent down and slowly closed Evans's eyes. She'd lost soldiers from other fireteams before, but never her own. Not since taking command of Sigma. She didn't much like how it felt.

But there wasn't time for sentimentality. There wasn't time for guilt or despondency, either. So they left his body lying between the two sets of shuddering doors without further word, and got running.

They had a mission, and Ginger would be damned if they weren't going to complete it.

CHAPTER TWELVE

Duke checked the blood splatter on the wall. It was little bigger than an old fifty pence coin, but it was fresh enough to still be dripping. It was from that flying stinger-bug they clipped, all right.

"At least we've got a trail to follow," he said, peering out past the end of the corridor. "This way."

Duke led Ginger and Ghost into the smoky chamber of yet another chimney. The stairwell in this one was rather more intact than the half-collapsed ladder in the first, at least, and a damn sight sturdier than the wooden set leading up through the mine shaft. Iron. Bolted to the inner circumference of the onyx chimney in which it stood. And it only headed up, which was a marked improvement.

She cast her gaze back down towards the cart interchange hall, double-checking that the roaches hadn't busted through the barricaded doors yet. Instead of a tidal wave of bugs, all Ginger saw was the inert body of Private Evans spread out in a pool of his own blood. She shut her eyes and inhaled deeply. She hadn't particularly liked the man and had enjoyed having him shoehorned into her squad even less, but the sight of him lying there still made her sick to her core. She was sorry to see any soldier go, especially one for whom she was responsible.

Plus, it was a reminder of what would happen to everyone in their company if they didn't make a hasty retreat.

Hell. Maybe it was already happening now.

"You know the higher we go, the further we have to come back down?" Ghost whispered to Ginger.

"That is generally how height works, yes."

"No, I mean... Those roaches are gonna flood the ground floor of the foundry in no time, you know? We probably ain't coming back this way. Which means we've gotta find another route down to base camp."

"Yeah, well. We'll cross that bridge when we come to it. You all right, Duke?"

He was staring up towards the top of the chimney with his rifle raised. Though he was hiding it well, Ginger could tell the cut across his thigh was hurting him. He winced with every other step.

"Yeah, I'm good. Bugs went up there, no question. Just gotta follow."

"Looks clear," Ghost added. "How do we know they didn't just fly all the way back into the nest?"

"We don't," Ginger replied. "But at least we can say we tried."

"Could just say it anyway, you know," Ghost mumbled to herself.

Duke led them slowly up the stairs. Each *clang* their boots made against the metal steps echoed up the chimney, yet they disturbed no bugs or birds. Either the stingers-on-wings were hiding in wait, or they were long out of earshot. Or vibration-shot, or however else their breed detected movement. One for the boffins in orbit, Ginger guessed.

"Another blood splatter," said Duke, gesturing to the rail running alongside the curving stairs with the tip of his rifle. "And a third a few metres further up. Looks like the bug was flapping all over the place. You must have hurt it bad, Ghost."

"Good."

"We keep following it," Ginger said, casting the barrel of her own rifle across the rings of empty balconies above. "As far as it goes."

They passed another two "clues" on their way to the top. One was dripping down the stone wall of the chimney as if the stinger-bug had drunkenly stumbled into it. The other was full of clumps and hanging off the lip of a step. The higher they climbed, the worse for wear the creature seemed to get.

Ginger was keenly aware this would have been more promising had the critter been hunting alone. As it was, any of the other flying scorpion things – or whatever else the queen had hiding inside the factory walls – could have snatched the sample off the dead bug's body. Still, it was worth a shot. Hopefully.

It was when the first flakes of snow drifted down from the grille above their heads that Ginger realised they were close to the end. Like the chimney down which they'd earlier jumped, a hinged grate lay at the very end of the stairwell. The rest of the chimney rose another twenty or thirty metres into the white sky. Ginger guessed the bugs they were after had fluttered out the top of it.

Duke unclipped the latches holding the grate in place, carefully pushed it open with his shotgun at the ready, and then exited onto the snowswept rooftop beyond.

It was the same rooftop as before, of course. Ginger recognised the other black chimney sprouting from the tundra, and the wide expanse of scorched rock in front of it where Duke had set off his incendiary grenades.

Oh, and also the swarm of flying roaches still circling the cloudy mountain peaks beyond. That was a dead giveaway, too.

"Psst." Duke waved them through. "Got a visual on the little buggers. Over there."

The two surviving stinger-bugs were bickering on top of a steam vent nearby. The one Ghost had shot was drenched in its own semi-luminous blood and missing one of its legs. The other kept jabbing at it like a crow pecking at a worm. Despite being fatally wounded, the first bug refused to give up the stolen canister it had gripped in its spindly claws.

Duke switched to his handgun and stalked forwards.

"Easy does it..."

They got within a few metres of the bugs without them noticing. Duke fired a single shot and took out the healthy one harassing the other, which tried to flutter to safety but couldn't lift itself off the ground. He marched closer, then swiftly executed it with a bullet to the head once he was sure he wouldn't hit the sample by mistake.

"I'll take that," he said, snatching the canister off the insect's leg and clipping it back onto his belt.

"They're not so driven by the hive-mind that they can't suffer pride," said Ginger, giving the dead bug a kick. "Looks like this little guy wanted to get the sample back to the queen himself."

"Or maybe the dumb bug just thought it looked pretty," Ghost replied impatiently. "Now, speaking of getting back..."

Sigma approached the edge of the rooftop. It was a hell of a long way down. The snowstorm had abated somewhat, and their view cleared. Ginger shook her head when she saw the way the marines were crowded around the base of the facility. Easy picking.

The way she saw it, they had two ways of getting back to the camp. Either they hurried down the helix staircase that wrapped around the inside of the chimney and hoped that the roaches didn't break through their door before the UEC's drill broke through theirs, or they risked navigating the treacherous mountain trail again. Though potentially far longer, the latter would have got Ginger's vote had it not been for the flying roaches still circling overhead. They'd never make it off the rooftop.

Three loud cracks went off from down in the camp below. The marines ducked as artillery rounds shot past the foundry and obliterated a few of the bugs buzzing through the airspace above.

"What the hell are they doing?" Duke grunted, uncrossing his arms from his head.

"The snowstorm must have blinded the UEC to aerial threats, and vice versa," Ginger hissed through gritted teeth. "Now the worst of it has passed, they probably want the skies clear before they take the facility."

"Good luck with that," said Ghost.

"Yeah, well, now we've got bigger problems." Ginger nodded up at the mountain peaks. "Look."

The artillery guns continued to tear holes in the roaches' ranks. Some of them shrieked and started dive-bombing the mounted guns. And, standing out in the open on the rooftop, Sigma was caught right in the middle.

"Oh, come on." Ghost's shoulders sagged. "Can't we *ever* catch a break?"

"Back down the chimney it is," said Duke, rushing back to the open grate.

"Ever get the feeling of deja vu?" Ginger asked Ghost, deadpan.

"Oh, not that way." Duke pulled back from the stairwell entrance with a face even stonier than the onyx chimney. "*Definitely* not that way."

Ginger pushed past him and looked over the side of the rusty stairwell barrier. A few roaches scuttled about down at the bottom of the chimney. None were rushing up the steps to kill them just yet, but it meant their hastily built barricade hadn't held. The whole ground floor had to be crawling with them by now.

"Mountain path it is, then."

"Yeah, think again." As the artillery guns below continued to boom, Ghost raised her sniper rifle and fired off a few shots at the swarm overhead. "We've got incoming!"

A couple of the flying roaches had split off from the dive-bombing masses, apparently having spotted an easier set of targets. Ghost took out one; Ginger and Duke's rifles tore through the other. Unfortunately, the noise of their self-defence only brought even more of the bugs towards them.

"We should have let the stupid sample go," Ghost muttered, shaking her head as they retreated further down the rooftop.

"Then we'd be dead down in the foundry instead of alive up here," Ginger snapped. "Well. Alive for a while longer, at least."

One of the artillery rounds dealt a glancing blow to the side of the chimney nearest them, blasting fragments of black stone across the width of the building. Sigma flinched and shielded their faces, then resumed taking pot-shots at the roaches coming their way.

Ginger was keenly aware they were running out of

rooftop almost as quickly as they'd run out of escape plans. Pushing forwards wasn't an option. As for backwards…

She glanced over her shoulder. Thick support cables of tightly-wound copper thread ran from each rear corner of the roof down to the very outskirts of the facility's perimeter. Relics from the foundry's unfinished construction, most likely. Their bronze colour reminded her of the Bridge of Etmark before they'd sent it crashing into the abyss.

"How's everyone's arms?" she asked.

Ghost scrunched up her face.

"*What?*"

"Better than my legs," Duke replied, raising one eyebrow. "That's for sure. Why?"

"Do you remember the assault course they had us run around in basic training?" Ginger replied. "It was inside an old aircraft hangar, but they'd put all sorts of trenches and trees in it?"

Ghost shot down another roach.

"Of course we do! Spit it out, Rogers!"

"We can use the support cable as a zip-line," Ginger growled frustratedly. "Our rifles should take our weight if we use them as handles. They might not fire all that well afterwards, but they'll hold."

"Jesus Christ, Ginger!" Ghost shouted. "Are you mental? The guns might hold, but that cable won't!"

"Yeah," Duke agreed, "that'll kill us for sure."

Ginger nodded at the swarm. No matter how many bugs the artillery guns took out, it didn't appear to grow any smaller.

"And staying up here *won't?*"

Ghost hesitated, then grunted in frustration as she hurried towards the pole onto which the nearest cable was fastened. She gave it a sharp kick, but it was too well embedded in the rock to budge.

"This is a bad idea too far," she said. "And this time, *you're* taking point. I don't give a crap about rank."

"Seriously? You really think you need to convince me to get off this rooftop first?"

Ginger stepped forward, reached up, and slung her rifle over the top of the cable. She wrapped the loose strap around each of her wrists for extra grip. Then she tugged on the rifle a few times, just to be safe. The cable held.

Duke fired off a couple of bursts behind her.

"Any time now..."

Ginger gritted her teeth, closed her eyes, and took a deep breath.

"You're only a few feet off the ground," she whispered to herself. "You're only a few feet off the ground..."

"Ginger!"

She grabbed onto her rifle as tight as she could and, with her eyes still scrunched shut, ran off the edge of the rooftop.

Her hands started slipping immediately. Every inch of her body suddenly felt as if it were made of tungsten, pulling the rest of her down. The screech of her rifle as it raced along the cable seemed to grow harsher with every second she was in the air.

But it was working. Somehow, it was actually *working*.

She hoped Ghost and Duke had the guts to follow. Ginger was the sergeant – it was her job to make sure her fireteam got off the roof safely. She should have gone last, not first. But this time she had to set an example.

A really stupid example, but a necessary one nonetheless.

The hood was whipped off her head. The freezing wind

slashed across her face like a fistful of razorblades. Her grip worsened. But she didn't dare open her eyes to see how much further she had to go – how much longer she needed to hold on for. She might have accidentally seen how far off the ground she was instead.

In the end, she had no choice. She could hear the UEC marines below her shouting something. Shooting something, too – perhaps the swarm above, hopefully not the horde on the other side of the factory's doors, and *really* hopefully not her. Though her eyes stung in the whistling wind, she finally took a look where she was going.

At first, a wall of white – there seemed to be little difference between the sky, earth or even the frozen waters beyond. Then she began to make out the icebergs floating in the distance, the transport trucks and hastily-erected Command tents, sparks spitting out from underneath her rifle... the icicle-blue outcrops of rock whizzing by beneath her feet.

Oh, and the pole to which the other end of the cable was tethered. At the speed she was travelling, her left and right halves would splatter to either side of it.

She needed to drop, and fast.

Ginger let go of her rifle and hoped the snow would cushion her fall. Unfortunately, the strap she'd wrapped around her wrists only tightened further. She was stuck hanging between the two ends of her firearm like a short-stringed marionette.

And the pole grew ever closer.

She only needed to get one hand free. Her left one felt the loosest, so she tucked her thumb into her palm hard enough to induce a cramp and then yanked and wriggled her wrist about as manically as she could.

It worked. The strap slipped over the fingers of Ginger's

left hand and the rifle flipped over the cable to her right. She tumbled forward for a good two or three seconds before burying herself a metre or so into the ground with a soft *thwump*.

This was followed by the clacking sound of half a dozen rifles being trained on her.

"I'm not a bug," she whimpered, face down.

"Do you need medical attention, ma'am?" one of the marines asked nervously.

"No," she groaned, crawling out of the snow. "I need to speak to Staff Sergeant Baker."

CHAPTER THIRTEEN

Ginger found Baker back at the same tent as when they'd left. Or at least, she thought it was the same tent. Base camp had changed quite a bit in the hours since their departure, with comm stations moved, new guard towers installed, and transporters with mounted guns brought in to form an armoured perimeter.

Up at the factory doors, the drilling continued.

"Christ, Sergeant." Baker rose from the cluttered desk at which he'd been working. "You look like hot death."

"Feel like it, sir." Ginger bent over double. "The bugs... you need to..."

"Catch your breath, Rogers. Where's the rest of your fireteam?"

"I don't..." Ginger turned and looked back the way she came. Her vision swam; she hadn't stopped to collect herself since she jumped onto the cable. "They should be..."

"Ah, there they are." Baker brightened slightly, but the fire in his eyes was short-lived. "I see Flores and Sampson, but no Evans...?"

Ginger blinked heavily, then permitted herself a tired

smile. Ghost had her arm around Duke and together they hobbled towards Baker's tent. They must have followed her down the makeshift zip-line as soon as they saw it was safe, but the gash in Duke's thigh made trekking across base camp slow work.

She turned back to Baker, then shook her head.

"Didn't make it, sir."

"Goddammit." He sighed. "Sorry to hear that. Did you get the sample?"

Ginger nodded at Duke as the two other members of Fireteam Sigma arrived under the flapping overhang of their tent.

"He's got it. But sir—"

"Let's see it, Private." Baker marched past Ginger and gestured for the canister. "Hand it over. Then get yourself over to the med tent. You look even worse than Rogers here."

Duke unclipped the sample from his belt and dumped it into Baker's open hand. He looked glad to be rid of it.

"Yes, sir. But, well, I really think you ought to hear what Rogers here has to say. Sir."

Staff Sergeant Baker turned back to Ginger with a harrowed look on his face.

"Something worse than losing a squad member, I take it?"

"Much worse," Ginger said in between bouts of coughing. "Losing the whole damn company, more like."

Baker looked both ways outside the tent to make sure nobody had overheard, then hurried everyone inside.

"You'd better have some good intel behind a statement like that," he said, delicately placing the canister upright on his desk and then collapsing into his folding chair. "I'm supposed to radio Command the second this sample gets in. Explain."

Ginger took a deep breath as she glanced across at Ghost and Duke. Ghost nodded to her encouragingly.

"We went right down to the bottom of the facility," she sighed, pointing at the sample, "and we found one of those cocoon sacs, just like that Intelligence guy said we would. Whole place was pretty much empty, though. We probably should have took that as a warning, hightailed it outta there when we had the chance. That's when we found her, sir. That's when we found the queen."

"Queen?" Baker's face turned grey. "What do you mean, *queen?*"

"We mean the brain behind the whole damn bug army," Ghost snapped. "That's what she's been trying to tell you!"

"And it's here?" Baker pointed to the tarpaulin under his feet. "Right now?"

"Yes, sir," Duke replied with a wince.

"And you geniuses didn't think to *kill it?*"

"Oh, we did our best," Ginger laughed sarcastically. "She's not your normal bug, sir. You're gonna need a nuke to take that bitch out. But that's not all. She spoke to us. Told us her plans."

"Bullshit. You're having me on."

"Wish I were, sir. Does it using pheromones or psychic waves, or something." Ginger shook her head. "But that's not the point! She knew we were coming. Made getting set up here easier than it should have been. The roaches have us surrounded, sir. This whole mission is one big trap. We have to stop drilling and get everyone out of here."

Baker stared at her, then turned his eyes to Ghost and Duke.

"No, she didn't hit her head," said Duke, shrugging. "That really is what the big bug told us."

"You can't be..." Baker pinched the bridge of his nose.

"The bugs aren't as stupid as some people think, I'll give you that. But military strategists?" He paused as if recalling the ambushes at Etmark and Rhinegarde. "Let's say I believe you, and this wasn't just some group hallucination brought on by subterranean fumes, or whatever. How the hell am I supposed to pass this info up the chain of command, Sigma? They'll think I'm a goddamn lunatic!"

"What Command thinks of you won't matter once the roaches start pouring through the factory doors!" Ginger pointed at the canister. "We got the sample for them, didn't we? Surely that gives what we're saying some credibility... right?"

Baker glared at them, then sighed and picked up his data pad.

"I need to report in about the sample. We'll see what they say about the rest."

As Baker opened a comm channel with his superior, Ginger turned to her fireteam.

"I wish Jackson was still with us," Duke grunted. "He'd know what to do."

"Probably recite an encyclopaedia entry on how to stop a queen from talking to the rest of her hive, or something," Ghost muttered. "At least we don't have to hear him say, *I told you so*."

"Major? It's Baker." Their staff sergeant rose from his chair and circled his desk. "Yes, they're back... Yes, they got it. But sir... I understand. Yes. But you really... Yes, sir. Right away."

Baker disconnected comms. Ginger raised an eyebrow.

"Well *that* sounded like it went well."

"Technically, it did." Baker grabbed the canister and led them all back outside. "Command's pleased. They want this stuff shipped up to the labs pronto."

"They need to evacuate the whole lot of us, Baker, not just the one bloody sample!"

"Watch yourself, Sergeant." Baker stopped short. "You're still on active duty, so act like it. The wrong person hears you talking like that and, well, it won't matter what you've done for the UEC."

He softened.

"Let's get you three to Major Adebowale. Then you can say your piece, if he lets you."

They got walking towards the major's tent again. It was at the opposite end of the camp somewhere, past the factory doors and the truck-mounted machinery trying to break through them. As they stomped across the sheets of metal and strips of tarpaulin laid over the snow, the drilling grew louder. Ginger tried her best to ignore it, even covering her ears as she passed, but the gnawing sense that their company was digging its own destruction grew too much to bear. She stopped and grabbed one of the marines close to the back of the vehicle.

"You've got to stop drilling," she screamed over the top of the shrill din. "There are roaches on the other side. Thousands of them. Switch the damn thing off!"

"Sergeant Rogers!" Baker marched back down the walkway towards her with a face as hot and red as a chilli pepper. "What the hell do you think you're doing? That's not your call!"

"Ah, sod it." Duke cupped his mouth with his hands and yelled, "There's a whole nest in there! You open those doors and we're all dead meat!"

"Well *this* isn't gonna get us court-martialled or anything," Ghost mumbled uneasily.

The engineers around the drill stopped what they were doing, though the drill itself continued to chisel away at the last layer of gunk encasing the twin doors. The marine sitting up front leaned out of the truck cabin's window. Another, most likely the ranking officer, looked up from her data pad in frustration.

"What the hell's going on here?" she yelled.

"Carry on, Sergeant," Baker shouted, dragging Ginger away. "Rogers, report back to my tent this instant. Flores, Sampson – you, too. I'll decide what to do with you after I—"

Everyone jumped as the drill broke through the factory doors with a crack like a suspension bridge cable snapping in two. The stone around them crumbled away in chunks; the gunk broke apart as if it were made of sand. The driver in the truck cab switched off the machinery and, following a long, sad whine, all was eerily silent.

And then the bugs came flooding through.

"Holy Christ," said Baker, mouth agape. "Everyone fall back!"

The front of the truck was lost in a wave of twitching legs and snapping mandibles. The driver tried to open the door but the roaches had it blocked. One smashed its way through the glass a second later. Blood splashed down the side of the cab.

Everyone in the camp grabbed their rifles and started shooting. They were lucky that the broken doorway only allowed half a dozen roaches through at a time. Even so, the truck with the drill was quickly overcome. One roach climbed onto the roof and released a blood-curdling screech into the air before being blasted back down by a nearby soldier.

"Fall back!" another staff sergeant ordered, running out from a neighbouring tent. "Find defensive positions! We've all dealt with nests before – you know what to do!"

But no sooner had this been said than a new terror gripped the fleeing soldiers. A tidal wave of roaches had risen up the chimneys and spilled over the top of the factory roof. They ran down its stone exterior like rain down an autumn window.

The bugs were coming faster than the marines could shoot.

There will always be more.

"Yep," said Ginger, backing away slowly. "We're all going to die."

CHAPTER FOURTEEN

Ginger sprinted away from the factory with one of Duke's arms draped over her shoulders. His other was wrapped around Ghost. The gash in his leg had weakened him – it didn't look infected, but it certainly pained him to walk. Normally Ginger would have taken him to the med tent. Given their present circumstances, she'd settle for somewhere quiet to administer the morphine from her own med kit instead.

"This is fine," Duke grunted, crashing onto an empty equipment crate. "I can help keep 'em back from here."

The roaches still swarmed through the hole in the foundry doors, joining the tide of those rushing down the outside walls. The truck with the drill was now utterly lost under their writhing bodies, as were about half a dozen marines too close to the building when the bugs broke out. Almost every remaining soldier in the camp had left their station in a bid to hold them back.

"Make this quick, Ginger," said Ghost, her submachine gun raised. Duke raised his own rifle alongside her.

Ginger squatted down next to Duke and rifled through

her satchel of medical supplies. They only carried the basics out in the field – bandages, scissors, gauze swabs, that sort of thing – but they had morphine ampules for when the wounds proved particularly bad. She'd more often seen it administered to soldiers who were otherwise going to die in agony, their guts spilling out of their belly from a roach bite. In Duke's case she simply wanted him numb and back onto his feet.

She checked the wound. It could have been infected, for all she knew, but it wasn't gangrenous. It wasn't dripping pus yet, it didn't smell, and most of the blood was dried. Good enough for her. She jabbed the morphine into Duke's thigh and then tossed the empty syringe into the snow.

"Woah." Duke shook his head as the drug entered his bloodstream. "Okay. Let's go kick some roach arse."

"Yeah, sure." Ghost helped Ginger drag Duke back onto his feet. "Anyone got a plan on how to do that?"

Ginger opened comms through her helmet.

"Baker, do you read me? Staff Sergeant, are you there?"

"Sergeant Rogers?" came Baker's breathless reply. "Where the hell are you? Regroup this instant. We need you here."

A roach scuttled down one of the makeshift walkways ahead of them, twitching its bulbous head this way and that as it searched for prey. A marine who hadn't even had time to put on his thermal jacket rushed out from the tent next to it and blasted the bug into the ground.

"Where is here, exactly?" Ginger shouted.

"Frontlines, just to the left of the facility doors," Baker replied. "I'm with fireteams Papa and Victor. Staff Sergeant Kimathi is down. Get back here and give us some supporting fire."

"Yes, sir."

The message was broadcast to all three members of Fireteam Sigma – they didn't need to pass so much as a word or glance between them to start running towards the action together. It would have been almost impossible to hear each other over the noise, anyway. There wasn't a millisecond not occupied by the sound of gunfire, and the mounted guns on the transporters now unloaded everything they had at the advancing horde – standard artillery, anti-aircraft rounds, even a couple of rockets. Fragments of rock the size of firetrucks were blasted off the factory walls as all hope of capturing the structure was quickly abandoned.

By the time they arrived close to where they'd stood when the doors first opened, the entire front of the camp was overrun. Bug and marine body parts alike dripped off the neighbouring tents – those not reduced to tattered flags waving in the winter wind, that is, or set alight by trash-fires overturned in the panic. Roaches raced down the path of tarpaulin towards them. Sigma emptied their magazines in their direction. Unable to pass, they stomped a sluggish detour through the thick snow behind the frontmost tents instead.

Ginger checked her rifle quickly. Its paint was long ruined anyway, and her trip down the makeshift zip-line had carved an ugly groove against the side of the upper receiver, but it seemed to fire just as well as ever. Right now, that's all she cared about.

She gingerly peered out past the other end of the tents where the rifle fire was loudest, the whole time expecting a roach to leap out and bite her face off. When it didn't, Ginger led Ghost and Duke out into the chaotic clearing on the other side. They were slap bang in the middle of the UEC frontline. Or what was left of it, at any rate.

Staff Sergeant Baker was crouching behind a barricade of sandbags alongside a bunch of other marines. As with the half a dozen other barricades, most of the privates were standing up and firing over the top. Roaches weren't exactly the type to hunker down; if they didn't constantly apply pressure, the marines would quickly be overrun.

Ginger sprinted over as soon as she saw him, pausing only long enough to eradicate a couple of stray bugs who'd found a way past the torrent of lead.

"Good of you to come back," Baker said, nodding towards the foundry. "This the trap you kept banging on about?"

"I'll be honest, Baker." Ginger ducked as shrapnel thudded into the other side of their barricade. "I don't think we've seen the half of it yet."

"I hope not. We've seen worse, though not by much."

"Are you talking about Rhinegarde, sir?" asked a baby-faced marine to Baker's right. "Because, erm, didn't we retreat from that? Sir?"

"And we can't go back and blow it up from the inside, either," Duke grunted enthusiastically. He was evidently feeling the benefits of the morphine. "Not this time, sir."

"Goddammit." Baker sighed and inspected what remained of fireteams Papa and Victor. "You might be right. We've got wounded who need to be evacuated and sooner or later, we're gonna run out of ammo. Or marines. Whatever happens, hold this line. I'm gonna reach out to the major."

Ginger, Ghost and Duke stood up and started firing at the horde. It was relentless. More than thirty marines formed the frontline, and mounted GAU-19 machine guns sprayed streams of rounds over their heads. And still it wasn't enough to keep a few roaches from breaking through.

"Major? This is Staff Sergeant Baker, do you copy? We've

got marines in need of evac and we're close to losing the north quadrant. What are our orders, sir?"

Ginger ducked as a grenade went off ahead of them. When she rose again, she spotted a line of marines in flame-retardant hazmat suits march past them with flamethrowers strapped onto their backs. She focussed on taking out the roaches in front of them. If there was one thing she knew from experience, it was that roaches did *not* like fire.

The flamethrower specialists hosed down the advancing swarm with jets hot enough to make Ginger's eyes water. The roaches backed away – those not instantly incinerated at the front, that is – and tried spilling around the sides instead. Those coming up from the rear clambered over and got tangled amongst those retreating. And still the specialists kept marching forward, their wall of flame pushing the roaches back towards the foundry doors.

"Understood, sir." Baker grabbed his rifle and called out to the surrounding fireteams. "Evac is a-go. Command considers the facility lost and will commence an orbital strike once we're no longer danger-close. They're sending in a bird for the sample. Everyone else is to fall back to the transporters on the west flank."

"Why the hell does the sample get a drop ship all to itself?" Ghost asked, incredulous. "Why not the whole company?"

"Because the skies are still too dangerous," Baker answered absent-mindedly. "And the sample's more important than us, that's why. Everybody, fall back!"

The surviving marines rose from behind the barricades and retreated gradually, concentrating their fire on the roaches managing to escape the growing inferno. Most of the bugs scuttling down the factory walls had splintered off and now stumbled through the dense snow on the mountainside instead. A small contingency of medics transferred a pair of badly injured marines onto stretchers and hurried them away. Those still able to walk had to hobble with the help of their squad mates.

A screech directly above made everyone look up. A lone flying roach had evaded the artillery cannons; it snatched up the marine beside Baker with its mandibles and dragged her screaming into the air, blood streaming from her sides as it clamped down hard. She clenched in pain and accidentally fired her rifle twice, shooting a member of her own fireteam first in the arm and then the throat. He died gurgling incoherently. A heavy round from one of the mounted guns nearby caught the roach square in its thorax, and both it and its unfortunate prey finally crashed to the ground behind the next tent over.

"Stay alert, people," Baker shouted, leading them further into the camp. "This ain't over until we're all dead or tucked up warm in our bunks, you hear me?"

Other fireteams were evacuating all around them. Or attempting to, rather. It was hardly a straight shot to the transporters. With roaches leaping out from collapsed tents and fires blocking off direct paths and panicked bullets flying in every direction, it was hard to even know which way they were supposed to go.

"Stick together," Ginger screamed to Duke and Ghost. "The smoke's getting thicker. It'll be too easy for one of us to get turned around."

A soldier was firing a mounted machine gun from on top of an armoured truck nearby. A pair of roaches climbed up the side of a neighbouring guard tower and leapt across. The soldier ploughed a few fifty calibre rounds into the roach in front while the other bug bit down hard on his neck and shoulder from behind. Ginger killed it with a few well-placed shots from her rifle, but it was too late for the marine. He slumped forward onto the gun and its long barrel tilted up towards the sky.

"Jesus Christ," Ghost moaned. "This is gonna be a goddamn slaughter."

"We'll make it out," Ginger replied. "We have to."

A drop ship just for the sample. Ginger gritted her teeth just thinking about it. How the hell could anything that small be so important? It was just a tube of bloody gunk. It didn't *do* anything. What did the scientists off-world expect to find out from it? The secrets behind mutating genetic code, perhaps? Or did they plan on doing something really stupid, like cloning the freakin' queen?

She grunted deep in her throat. Hell, she knew why the sample was so important. It was simple really.

Because Command said it was, for all the difference it made to everyone actually down on the ground.

There. The transporters. Ginger spotted about a dozen of them parked at the western edge of the camp. Baker was leading what remained of their three fireteams towards one tucked under the overhang of a rocky outcrop. Its engine was rumbling idly, the driver hanging out the door of her cabin and waving desperately for her passengers to hurry up. She'd dropped the ramp at its rear in anticipation. Other transporters were already full of marines and preparing to set off for the empty tundra.

No sign of that bloody drop ship, though.

"Fireteams Sigma, Papa and Victor," Baker yelled through the roar of their engines, "you go on ahead. I'll stay back until the bird arrives for the sample."

"Are you serious?" Ginger shook her head. "You can't stay here! Just get the damn ship to come to you!"

"Orders are orders, Sergeant." Baker shrugged and

gently tossed the canister in his hand. "Besides, you know me. I'll take any excuse to leave this godforsaken rock I can get."

Fireteam Victor had rushed ahead, transfixed by the allure of the open truck. Suddenly, a hailstorm of chitin rounds tore through the clearing. One marine made it to the safety of the transporter without injury; another was caught in the leg but managed to hobble into the back of the vehicle after him. The other two members of the fireteam had their flesh sheared quite literally from their bones.

"Goddammit!" Ginger screamed, grabbing Ghost before she could push further forward. "Mutant bugs! Everyone get into cover!"

They threw themselves behind another lump of blueish-grey rock jutting out from the snow just as a second barrage of chitin rounds sprayed between them and the trucks. A not-insignificant percentage of the brittle projectiles seemed to shatter on the other side of their cover.

"For crying out loud," Duke grunted. "I thought we killed all of them getting up here!"

"Apparently not," Baker snarled. "Flores, do you have a visual on the bugger?"

Ghost leaned out of cover just long enough to peer down the line of transporters before a third onslaught began to rain down on their rock. She pulled her head back and let out a gasp of frustration.

"There are two of them," she replied, deadpan. "Where the hell are they even coming from?"

"Can you take them out?" Baker asked.

"Maybe if I got to a vantage point without them seeing me," Ghost replied uneasily, "but lining up a shot with them suppressing us like this? No chance, sir."

The first set of transporters was starting to leave. The

driver of the truck Sigma had been sprinting towards gestured impatiently. Staff Sergeant Baker reluctantly waved her on.

"What are you doing, sir?" asked one of the surviving marines from Fireteam Papa. "That's our ride out of here!"

"You want to try running to it? Be my guest. There's no use in keeping it here when we can't get to it. May as well get as many people out as—"

Baker was cut off as the whole world turned upside down. It sounded as if the very fabric of the universe was being ripped in half – an explosion so thunderous, so pained and so drawn out that Ginger almost believed Command had nuked their site from orbit.

For the slightest sliver of a second, the snow-blanketed ground beneath the rumbling transporters appeared to fold in on itself. Then suddenly it ruptured upwards in a row of colossal, rocky geysers. Three of the transporters were tossed into the air as if they weighed nothing. They came crashing down to the earth on their backs with their sides buckled inwards and their wheels still spinning.

Tank bugs lumbered out from the cratered wreckage with the steady ferocity of a vanguard of war elephants. Perhaps it was only due to her position sprawled out on the ground, but Ginger was sure they were even bigger than the previous monstrosities she'd gone up against. Each step of their six legs sank half a dozen feet into the earth. And from between those legs emerged even more roaches, flooding out from secret ambush-holes underground.

"Now *that*," Ginger murmured to Baker, "is the trap."

A bloody driver tried to crawl free from one of the upturned transporters through its cabin window. The ramp at the vehicle's rear remained locked shut, though Ginger had her doubts any of the marines trapped inside were still in any shape to leave anyway. The driver was almost out when one of the tank bugs stomped down on it, crushing both her and the truck in half.

"Fall back to the south-east," Baker yelled, rising to his feet and hurriedly ushering his remaining fireteams back the way they came.

"But there's nothing past that 'cept the sea," one of the other privates shouted. "We'll be sitting ducks!"

"I know," Baker said, nodding resignedly. Ginger waited for him to follow this up with something charged, something inspirational. He looked her in the eye.

"I know," was all he could add.

CHAPTER FIFTEEN

Lieutenant Tom Quimby piloted his *Sparrowhawk* class gunship through the thin sheet of cloud towards the mountain facility. It was a small plane – though it was suitable for limited space travel, Quimby couldn't think of it as anything else – and he was its sole occupant. The mission required a quick in-and-out.

His orders were to extract the sample and return to the *UECS Invincible*. That was it. No marines were to get on board, no matter how bad things were on the ground. Lethal force was authorised. Though he supposed he'd let whomever was holding the canister ride along, if it helped expedite the process.

The full scale of the disaster below was apparent the moment Quimby's gunship broke cloud cover. He'd been briefed to expect the worst, but his breath still caught in his throat at the sight of it. A third of the tents in the camp appeared to be on fire, and that was the least of everyone's problems. Roaches poured out from the industrial structure like turgid water from a broken drain, and the only viable route for a land-based evacuation was blocked by a wall of tank bugs bigger than his ship.

Effed-up beyond all recognition, indeed.

"Got a visual on the base," he said into comms. "Making my descent now, over."

"Roger that, Lieutenant," came the relaxed voice on the other end of the line.

No sooner did he cut comms than an explosive egg sac got launched from the other side of the mountain range. Quimby banked sharp left out of the sac's path with ease. His *Sparrowhawk* was considerably more nimble than the bulky drop ships they used to transport troops.

A lone orbital strike obliterated the bug cannon a second later. A great cloud of snow burst upwards and one of the mountain peaks collapsed in on itself. Quimby wondered how long Command would wait after the sample was extracted before bombarding the whole camp. It was basically already lost. They weren't doing the marines down there any favours.

"Thank you, Command," he said, letting out the breath he was holding. "I owe you one. Continuing my... Hold on. I've got visual on a bogey, twelve o' clock."

A dark stream rose up from the wreckage of the cannon, growing into an aerial mass like a ball of wool unspooling in reverse. It spread out to blacken the already sunset sky.

Not one bogey. A whole swarm.

"Oh, Christ." Quimby hurriedly flicked a row of overhead switches to bring the ship's primary guns online. "There's thousands of them. Engaging now!"

"Negative, Lieutenant," Command replied less casually than before. "Retrieving the sample is priority one. Focus on—"

Quimby didn't register what Command said next. The

flying roaches spilled across the sky towards him, quickly devouring the view outside his cockpit window. He squeezed the triggers and tore through the bugs in front of him with his gunship's Vulcan cannons. A few roach bodies splattered against the nose of his ship while others veered off. He felt the onboard computers fight to keep the plane stable, and then he was out the other side – nothing but sky and snow-tipped peaks ahead of him.

"I've lost visual," he barked into comms. "Sweeping round for another..."

His words stopped but his mouth kept moving as he caught sight of the bug-flock again. They were on a collision course with his right flank. And they were coming in fast.

"Oh, sh—"

Quimby tried banking, but it was too late. The roaches crashed into the side of the gunship, pulling it into the swarm with them, slashing at it with their claws and pincers. The glass of his cockpit windows started to crack.

Something in the wing blew out. An alarm went off.

He felt the *Sparrowhawk* tip down.

GINGER WATCHED the gunship barrel downwards, smoke billowing from the turbojets under its wings. Roaches were still crawling over its exterior panels when it crashed into the side of the mountain.

The explosion was loud enough to interrupt even the cacophony of chaos down on the ground. Bright enough, too – the resulting flash doubled the light provided by the growing pockets of fire around the base camp. Just to make their odds of survival even worse, evening was settling in.

Fireteam Sigma had retreated to an overturned tactical

truck and were holed up with Staff Sergeant Baker, plus a couple more squads with whom they'd managed to regroup. Advancing tank-bugs and a steady barrage of chitin rounds continued to push them towards the south-east. A line of shipping containers by the icy shore roughly sixty metres behind them marked the UEC's last defensive line.

"So much for getting *this* out of here," Baker grunted, begrudgingly pocketing the canister.

Ghost screamed in frustration and opened fire around the side of their cover.

"Good to know this was all for nothing, sir."

"Keep it together, Private. Don't count us out just yet."

Ginger poked her head out past one of the truck's tyres. She caught sight of one of the mutant bugs, its face warped into a perpetual snarl. She pulled herself back into cover before its chitin rounds could turn her head into a spiky sea urchin, then suppressed a shiver. To think they used to be Essyen. To think they were civilised, once. To think the same fate might happen to *them*.

"Heads up," Duke shouted. He pointed above the facility. "Bugs ain't the only problem we've got to deal with."

The gunship crash had set off a small avalanche; a tide of white powder raced down the side of the mountain towards the factory's chimneys, drowning all in its path. So far it was doing the UEC a favour – the casualties were exclusively roaches spilling out from inside the foundry – but who knew how far into the camp the snowslide might come.

"Bloody hell," Baker sighed. "How's our flank looking, Fireteam Papa?"

"Holding off the roaches fine, sir," Sergeant Richards shouted from the other end of the truck, "but we ain't putting so much as a dent in those shamblin' freaks."

"And we can't fall back any further until they're dealt with." Baker shook his head. "No use in calling the major. He's already at the water's edge. He'd only lose more marines trying to help us."

Ghost elbowed Ginger, then pointed up at an empty guard tower nearby. Though its base was skirted by a few feet of flame, it was one of the few vantage points in the camp still upright.

"Remember Rhinegarde?" she asked, swallowing hard. "If you can keep those mutants distracted, I might be able to get up there and take one or two of them out. Then the rest of you'll have a window in which to retreat."

Ginger flinched as a rocket-propelled grenade whistled over the top of their heads, spun around in the air wildly, and then crashed into the side of a lumbering tank bug. It sank to one knee – or whatever disgusting excuse for a joint its species had – then lifted its horned head and continued bulldozing through the outer reaches of the camp unperturbed.

"It's worth a shot," Ginger replied. "You make sure to jump to safety once we're clear, got it? Snow should cushion your landing. Everyone else get that?"

"Provide covering fire," Sergeant Richards replied, nodding to Baker. "On your signal, sir."

"Good. Ready, Private Flores?"

Ghost nodded.

"Okay. Now!"

Everybody leaned as far out from the upturned tactical truck as they dared. There was no use in trying to suppress the bugs – the roaches were too vicious and the mutants were either too dumb or too numb to notice. But with or without the queen's influence, they weren't *that* smart. If you peppered them with enough ammunition, they weren't much inclined to look anywhere else.

Ghost sprinted out from cover with her shoulders hunched and her head down. Her sniper rifle swung loosely over her back. She vaulted over a bench and then skipped through the dancing flames without a moment's hesitation. Ginger released her trigger and darted back into cover the second she saw Ghost set foot on the bottom rung of the guard tower's ladder.

She checked on the rest of their squad. No fatalities, miraculously. One member of Fireteam Papa had a fresh gash across her upper arm, but she was taking it like a champ, still firing at the advancing bugs even after her sergeant had given the order to return to cover.

The mutants didn't seem to notice Ghost making the climb. The tower was only four or five metres tall, so thankfully it didn't take long for her to reach the top and rest her rifle against the lip of the barrier.

She let off her first shot only seconds later. Baker and Ginger watched as the mutant bug closest to them collapsed to the floor, a bloody crater where its disfigured face used to be. Then she fired again – a turbulent boom that seemed to hang in the air a moment longer than it should – and the second mutant stumbled long enough for Ghost's third round to sheer the top of its skull clean off.

"That's our window," Baker shouted, gesturing past Ghost's guard tower. "Everyone, fall back to the water!"

Ginger didn't need to be ordered twice. She joined Duke in sprinting out of cover just as Ghost had done, surrounded by a crowd of marines she didn't recognise. Some had been taking cover elsewhere and saw the opportunity. They weren't completely in the clear – more than a few soldiers went down under a fresh spray of chitin rounds, and one man got disembowelled by a roach hiding amongst the ruins of the med tent – but most made it to the comparative safety of the waterfront defensive line. Ginger only realised she had her eyes scrunched shut in terror when she almost tripped over a body sprawled out on the floor.

She threw Duke and herself behind one of the large, corrugated supply containers and then turned back to Ghost's watch tower.

"Ghost, we're clear," she screamed up at her. "Get down—"

It was as if Ghost knew what was coming next. She didn't even reach for the ladder. For a split second, all she seemed to do was look fondly at the two friends with whom she'd trained and travelled the stars.

Then an egg sac, launched from the back of one of the tank bugs, careened into the tower. It erupted on impact. When Ginger stopped shielding her eyes from the sudden flash of green, the tower was nothing but a charred, lopsided husk.

"No," Duke mumbled beside her. "No, no, this isn't right..."

"Ghost?" Ginger felt utterly lost. *"Ghost!"*

"Oh, God." Staff Sergeant Baker pulled Ginger back into cover before any of the incoming chitin rounds could hit her. "Get it together, Sergeant Rogers. You hear me?"

"She's gone, Baker..."

"Survive now, mourn later." He shoved Duke in the shoulder. "Don't let Private Flores's sacrifice go to waste, got it?"

Duke nodded stupidly.

"Yeah, I... Yes, sir."

"Good. Both of you, follow me."

They hurried after Baker as he led them through the

camp's final set of defences. If they could really be called that. Nobody had thought to factor in a bug ambush when setting up the camp, and technically they were fleeing right out the other side of it. The large, metal supply containers formed a convenient – though hardly airtight – perimeter wall, and the surviving marines' defences consisted of whatever they could hastily erect outside it. Sandbags, dismantled ammo crates – someone had even stuck a detached transporter door upright in the snow. Nothing that could stop the horde.

What was the point, Ginger wondered? She passed the other marines desperately running to cover in a drugged, daydream haze. Everyone was just going to die anyway.

The ocean lashed against the ice and snow. A fine, salty mist drifted over the battlefield. The air was so bitter, Ginger felt as if her cheeks would crack open and the blood inside freeze into ruby rivers. She knew that if she were to try swimming to freedom, she'd be dead before she even reached the first iceberg.

It wasn't like she had the energy left, anyway.

Baker found Major Adebowale crouching behind a temporary barrier right down by the shore. They shared a curt nod as he, Ginger and Duke fell into cover beside him.

"Extraction was a no-go," Baker said, holding out the canister.

"Yes, I figured." Adebowale nodded at the fiery wreckage up on the mountain. "I've been trying to reach Command. They told me they would send reinforcements."

Ginger looked up at the empty sky.

"Funny," she replied. "I don't see any."

But the sky wasn't clear for long. A megaton of dynamite seemed to go off inside the mountain. As a fountain of rock and snow blew upwards, Ginger genuinely believed they'd been fighting in the shadow of a volcano instead. That would be just their luck. But then she saw the great, dark mass rise from inside – not magma, not another swarm of roaches, but a single carapaced bug. She flew on moth wings the size of drop ships and behind her trailed tendrils as long as a Boeing 747. Bomber bugs, plus a new breed Ginger didn't recognise, followed and flanked her like an insect fighter squadron.

"Mother of God," Major Adebowale whispered. "What is that?"

"The queen," Ginger grunted defeatedly. "She's been holed up here ever since her asteroid struck millennia ago. I guess she's looking for a safer neighbourhood."

"We need an orbital strike this second," Major Adebowale barked into his reinforced data pad. "Command, do you read me? *Command?* God help us..."

Duke slumped against the barrier and stared out at the crashing waves.

"I can't believe she's gone..."

Three sounds dominated the world beyond the container wall. First, the shrill bursts of automatic turret fire. Second, the screech of the roaches as they were cut down. And third, the endless hailstorm of chitin rounds puncturing the corrugated metal like a thousand office workers' punch-cards. Every now and then a roach or two would get through, and the last remaining flame-specialists would push them back.

The tank bugs gradually loomed over the top of their makeshift barricade. Soon they would break through. Anyone not yet inside the barricade was surely dead already.

"For crying out loud." Ginger readied her rifle. "They may as well just nuke the whole site and get it over with."

Staff Sergeant Baker took aim beside her.

"You're probably right, Rogers. Still. Let's not make it easy for them, eh?"

"Sentry guns are depleted," screamed a marine camped on top of the wall. "Here they come!"

Roaches spilled through the gaps between containers; where there was no more room to fit through, they scurried over the top in a twitching, nauseating flood. The marines with flamethrowers hosed their fiery jets at the openings, but there were too few specialists and too many angles of attack, and they were quickly lost amongst the swarm.

"Open fire!" screamed Major Adebowale.

Not that anyone had needed the order. The majority of the remaining marines had started shooting the second the bugs breached the perimeter. A few froze in a petrified stupor. One even ran backwards from his post as if he preferred to try his luck with the sea. Nobody stopped him.

Ginger pulled the trigger again and again, letting off controlled bursts of three rounds at the myriad targets. At least it wasn't hard to hit something. Duke was upright now, too. He'd switched his rifle to fully automatic and was spraying rounds indiscriminately.

"I'm over here, you ugly bastards," he yelled above the din. "Come get some!"

The soldiers closest to the containers were quickly overrun. They died screaming. The roaches ripped their limbs off and flung them into the air like graduation mortar boards. More of the marines around Ginger lost their bottle at that point, hesitating or fleeing backwards.

"Hold your ground," the major shouted.

The first of the tank bugs reached the barricade seconds later. It stomped through one of the containers as if it were nothing but an empty cola can. Even more roaches scuttled through.

"I said, hold your ground!" the major repeated. "Desertion is a—"

Chitin rounds began to permeate the shore as mutant bugs lurched into the fray. One of the shards crashed ineffectively against Major Adebowale's helmet; another pierced his cheek and shattered his teeth. He fell backwards into the snow, blood pouring through his fingers as he clutched at his face.

"Jesus Christ," Ginger muttered to herself as she switched one magazine out for another. "Jesus *goddamn* Christ..."

"They just keep coming," Baker murmured beside her.

All but the last line of sandbags and upturned crates were lost. The more marines died, the quicker the onslaught progressed. There was no holding them back. There never had been.

Baker screamed as a roach leapt over their barrier and knocked the rifle out of his hands. He fell onto his back with the roach on top of him, snapping at his face with its mandibles and scratching at his chest with the claws at the end of its second, smaller pair of arms.

Ginger glanced over at him but couldn't afford to stop shooting at the bugs in front of her.

"Baker!"

The roach tore open Baker's stomach with its claws. His warm intestines spilled out and steamed in the snow. Baker screamed in agony and pulled his handgun out of its holster. Three bullets to the head sent the bug crashing to the ground beside him.

With a trembling, crooked hand, he unclipped the

sample's canister from his belt and tossed it into the snow next to Ginger.

"Make sure—"

The roaches swarmed him before he could finish his sentence. Ginger turned and fired at them, but it was too late. Baker was dead. And the roaches were everywhere. *Everywhere.*

She reached down and grabbed the sample.

Big mistake.

No sooner had she wrapped her fingers around the canister than a roach wrapped its mandibles around her left forearm. It clamped down hard just below the elbow. Bone crunched. Blood spurted. Ginger screamed.

Both of her hands tensed up from the pain. She emptied half of her magazine into the roach's thorax, but it only bit down harder in retaliation. Ginger watched in excruciating horror as her arm tore off and landed in the snow, still clutching the sample tight.

She toppled backwards with the dead roach on top of her. Ginger could barely think, barely *see*, it hurt so much. Bugs surged past, screaming and twitching their heads to and fro, but they didn't seem to notice her.

"Duke...?" she whispered groggily.

He was to the left of her, blasting roaches back with shotgun slug after shotgun slug. He looked like he was screaming at them, but Ginger couldn't hear him properly. The world was muted, submerged, and foggy around the edges.

She watched as three roaches piled onto Duke at once. He went down swinging and shooting. Ginger turned her head and moaned. She didn't need to see any more of her friends die today.

Something shot down from the sky and tore a hole

through the armoured shell of one of the tank bugs. It detonated from the inside, showering the battlefield with bloody insect chunks and blowing off a neighbouring tank bug's leg in the process. Then another explosion went off, and then another.

Orbital strikes from one of the battlecruisers, Ginger thought to herself as she faded out of consciousness. Too little, too late. Command in a bloody nutshell.

The ocean wind grew fierce, the rattle of rifle fire grew louder, and then everything turned to white.

CHAPTER SIXTEEN

Blinding white light blazed overhead.
Ginger opened her eyes and saw nothing.
Pain pulled her back under.

THE NEXT TIME GINGER WOKE, it was to an intersection of sound. The brash, staccato voice of a sergeant barking out orders. Electrical hums whining like tinnitus. The shrill whirring of fans and the harsh hiss of pistons. The glaring white sun above her remained, certainly – it reduced everything around her to a series of black, amorphous shapes. She lay there in its heat, though it seemed to her that all else in the world was very, very cold.

Still, it burned. Her skin, her eyes, her arm – everything. Ginger tried to get up, but the only things she succeeded at moving were her lips as she let out a whimpering groan.

"She's coming round," boomed a voice from somewhere near. "Better give her another ten milligrams of propofol."

"Are you sure, doctor?" replied somebody younger, less

authoritative. "We've already administered the maximum recommended dose."

"She can handle it. Besides, it's better than the alternative. She'll want to be asleep for this."

Ginger *did* want to be asleep. She felt like she hadn't slept properly in so long. Forever, maybe. And when the waking world was such a nightmare, a little dreaming every now and then didn't seem so bad...

Her breathing slowed, the pain grew dull, and she let herself slip down deeper.

"I BELIEVE the patient is regaining consciousness."

Ginger heard the voice, but it took a couple more seconds before she realised it was talking about her. She guessed she was no longer asleep. Shame. She'd been having quite a nice dream involving a log cabin and a waveless lake.

Groggily and begrudgingly, she opened her eyes.

She was lying in a hospital bed and covered up to her stomach with fuzzy covers. Squishy pillows propped up her head. It was hardly comparable to a suite in the Ritz-Carlton, but she couldn't remember the last time she'd actually lain on something softer than a breeze block. Not in her coffin-bunk on the *UECS Invincible*, that was for sure. Come to think of it, probably not since she'd been a kid.

The room was fairly unremarkable. No windows. Two automatic doors – one which Ginger presumed led to a washroom of some kind, and another connecting her room to the wider hospital. She could faintly hear people talking as they hurried back and forth outside. The lights weren't as bright as before. The air smelled strongly of antiseptic.

She tried talking. Her throat was parched, and the first few words came out as nothing but a dry wheeze. She cleared her throat, swallowed a couple of times, then tried again.

"Hello?"

"Good morning, Sergeant Rogers."

Ginger jerked upright as a white, plastic, barrel-shaped piece of apparatus emerged from the corner of the room and hovered beside her bed. Her right hand instinctively shot to her hip, but obviously there was no holster under the covers.

"What... the hell... are you?"

"Please do not be alarmed, Sergeant Rogers! I am the medical automata assigned to this ship. You may call me Doc, if you'd like."

"I'll call you much worse than that if you don't back the hell away from me," Ginger replied. "Where am I? And what are you doing here?"

"You are aboard the *UECS Invincible* where you are receiving medical treatment for the wounds you sustained during Operation Iron Nest," Doc answered cheerfully, floating a couple of feet backwards. "I apologise if my presence unsettled you, Sergeant Rogers. Your wellbeing is my utmost priority. I requested to oversee your recovery specifically."

Ginger groaned and scrunched up her eyes. Whatever painkillers they'd given her were wearing off.

"Why on earth would you do that?"

"Because you are a very important person, Sergeant Elizabeth Rogers, daughter of Jack and Amber Bishop! Your name got flagged on my systems the second the extraction team admitted you as a patient. Did you know that your father and I were on board the *Confession* together? He liberated me alongside many other automata. But I also liberated him!"

"Well, lucky you. You've probably spent more time with the guy than I have."

"Maybe!"

On top of her growing headache, Ginger's skin was starting to itch. She reached up with her right hand and scratched between her shoulder blades. But her left arm wouldn't budge. She could feel her fingers flexing, but the appendage itself seemed glued to the bed.

"Erm, RoboDoc?" Turning her head was a sluggish process. "Why can't I move my—"

All the lethargy left Ginger's body the instant she saw how Operation Iron Nest had left its mark. The bottom half of her left arm was gone, replaced with a black, mechanical hand built of pistons and gears. It was strapped tight to the side of her luxury gurney.

"Jesus Christ!" Ginger thrashed about, kicking off her bedcovers in the struggle. "Jesus *effing* Christ! What in God's name have you done to me?"

"You are in clear distress." A syringe shot out from inside one of Doc's many compartments. "Would you like me to give you some drugs?"

"No!" She swatted the needle away with her human hand. "I want you to give me my bloody arm back!"

"Regretfully that is not possible, Sergeant Rogers. Your arm was severed below the elbow, and exposure to sub-zero temperature snow cauterised the wound. Reattachment was not a viable option. Would you like me to call a licensed therapist?"

"I want you to get me a human, yes!"

At that moment a doctor burst through the automatic doors with a mildly alarmed look on his face. He hurried around the other side of her bed – the side with her pinned-down prosthetic.

"Apologies, Ms. Rogers. I only just got out of surgery." Ginger recognised his voice from back when she'd been drifting in and out of consciousness. "I'm Dr. Youssef. How are you feeling?"

"Bloody peachy! What the hell is *this?*"

"Please understand we did everything we could," the doctor replied. "Your arm was retrieved by the extraction team alongside the sample, and reattachment was the first thing we tried. It was in remarkable condition, considering."

"I explained about the cauterisation," Doc added enthusiastically.

"Yes, well." Dr. Youssef raised his bushy eyebrows. "It wasn't to be. You're fortunate we had Doc here. A lot of marines owe him their lives, in fact. The automata have helped advance our understanding of biomechanical prosthetics tenfold. We can replace arms, legs – even some major organs. Some patients even say it's an improvement."

"Being mechanical isn't all that bad," said Doc. "And it's only a little bit of you. You probably won't even notice!"

Ginger grumbled and tried to yank her arm free again.

"Why have you tied me down? I'm not under arrest, am I?"

"No, no, not at all," Youssef replied, fumbling at the buckles. "Patients tend to experience adverse reactions upon waking from operations they don't know they've had, that's all. But please, take it slow. You'll need some time to adjust."

Ginger raised her prosthetic arm in front of her as soon as the straps were loose. The obsidian-black metal glistened under the hospital lights with a plasticky sheen. The design was surprisingly simple, and each of the fingers flexed perfectly in accordance with her wishes. It was as if she'd always had a mechanical skeleton beneath, ever since birth – someone had simply peeled the skin off.

She shivered. Half of her felt nauseous, while the other half couldn't tear her eyes from it.

"You'll need to stay here another few days so we can keep a watch on you, make sure your body doesn't reject the prosthesis." Dr. Youssef returned to the doorway. "But all the signs are good. Oh, and you've got a visitor. He's been waiting outside for the past sixteen hours. We'll leave you to catch up."

"Pleasure to meet you, Sergeant Rogers," Doc said ecstatically, drifting out the door behind him. "If you need anything, please buzz me!"

The automatic doorway stood empty for a moment as if somebody was lingering on the other side. Ginger swallowed nervously. A visitor? On the *UECS Invincible*? She really hoped news of her brush with death hadn't reached Jack Bishop.

But the big, grinning face that emerged seconds later didn't belong to her father.

It belonged to Duke.

"Hey!" he said, sheepishly approaching the bed. "How's my favourite sergeant doing?"

"What?" Ginger spluttered and laughed in surprise. "How? I saw you go down. The roaches were all over you!"

"Yeah, man, and I've got the scars to prove it." Duke pulled down the neckline of his t-shirt to reveal a ghastly tapestry of raw flesh running across his shoulder. "Got an even bigger one on my hip, too. They had me undergo reconstructive laser-surgery for two days straight. Made that gash I got back in the foundry seem like a paper cut."

"But..."

"Couple of boys from Fireteam Papa blew the roaches

off me almost as quick as I went down," Duke explained. "*Almost* as quick," he added, nodding at his scars again. "Only about half a dozen marines made it out in total. You're not the only one missing a few bits, neither."

"Christ. Command waited long enough to send in reinforcements, didn't they?"

"Not reinforcements." Duke shook his head. "Just the one special ops fireteam. They couldn't risk sending another gunship, so they dropped a landing boat into the ocean. Came driving right up the shore. They weren't there to extract anything besides the sample, but we, erm, made a pretty convincing argument."

"And Baker?"

Duke shook his head.

"Damn it. I hope Command's bloody happy. Why do you think they wanted that stupid sample so bad, anyway?"

"Couldn't say. Something to do with the queen, maybe? I'm guessing we'll never find out. Don't make no difference, really."

"No, I guess not. Look, Duke… I'm sorry about Ghost. I know the two of you were close from the beginning."

"Thanks, Sarge. Hey, we all were. Not gonna feel right without her. But she wouldn't want us to mope, right? She'd probably punch us on the arm for getting all soppy."

"Would hurt her more than me." Ginger raised her prosthesis. "Look at this thing. I'm like a bloody T-800."

Duke grinned.

"Yeah, man. Badass. Wouldn't mind a pair myself."

"Pfft. Careful what you wish for."

"Right." Duke slapped his thighs and rose from her bedside. "I'm booked in for another round of laser treatment. We'll grab a drink and toast Flores properly after you get discharged, all right?"

"Make it five drinks and I might consider it."

"Get real. You couldn't handle three."

Duke paused in the doorway.

"Oh, and don't take too long getting back on your feet. We're being shipped planetside again at the end of the month."

"What?" Ginger sat bolt upright. "Us, in our condition?"

"Yeah, well. All hands on deck, right? Enjoy the rest."

The door hissed shut. Ginger consulted the digital calendar on the cabinet beside her bed and then collapsed back onto her pillow with a sigh. Wow. A whole eight days to recuperate and then back onto the front lines. Typical. As far as she was concerned, the time she'd spent unconscious didn't count as leave.

Ginger reached up, grabbed the button for the patient-controlled analgesia pump, and administered herself a fresh dose of morphine.

"Might as well get comfortable while I still can," she grumbled.

CHAPTER SEVENTEEN

Ginger shrugged on her fatigues. She supposed she should get used to calling them "field uniforms" now. Using the proper terms for everything was rather expected of her new rank.

She sighed and stared at her reflection above the bunk room sink. She didn't *feel* any different, no matter what the insignia on her collar said. She sure looked it, though. Gone was the fresh, bright-eyed face that once smirked back from the other side of the grubby tin mirror.

Much to Ginger's surprise, they'd put her right back in the same room on the *UECS Invincible* as when she first arrived at New Terra. No fancy dorms for the ranking officers, it turned out. She supposed it made sense. It wasn't as if humanity had any new young men and women to fill the empty ranks.

Speaking of empty ranks...

Ginger turned her eyes to the bunk behind her. Ghost's bunk a mere twelve months before. The pillow and bedsheets were tucked neatly at one end. An old, tattered photograph still clung to the cold, metal wall, one of its corners peeling backwards like a wilting flower. Some actress from the days when people still made movies, according to Ghost. She'd cut it out from an old-school magazine.

Bloody hell. Ginger shook her head. She still half-expected Flores to come barging in, complaining about the sludge they served in the mess hall and mocking her for being a lightweight. The galaxy didn't seem right without her. Scores of marines had been slaughtered down on New Terra, billions of lives had been lost back on Earth… and yet this was the first time Ginger felt as if the jigsaw of the universe was missing a vital piece.

A trio of heavy knocks shook the bunk room door. Ginger snapped upright.

"Yes?"

"Briefing's in ten," said Duke. "You coming?"

Ginger glanced at the clock on her bunk-side cabinet. Dammit. Turning up late to her own speech hardly gave the best first impression.

"Be right there."

She splashed some cold water on her face, dried herself off with an irritatingly abrasive hand towel, and then opened her bunk room door.

"Hey, Lieutenant." Duke smiled at her from the other side. "Big day today. You nervous?"

"What do you think?" Ginger stepped into the narrow corridor and shut the door behind her. "I feel like I'm gonna throw up a kidney. How the hell did Baker do this?"

"Because he was a good man who truly cared about the marines under him." Duke elbowed her affectionately in the ribs. "But hey, what would he know? You're gonna be in charge of twice as many people now."

"Oh, God. Don't remind me. This promotion's a joke. I couldn't even keep everyone in my bloody fireteam alive."

"Hey." Duke stopped and put his hand on Ginger's shoulder. "Don't talk like that. Ghost's death wasn't your fault. Neither was Evans's. Just the way war goes, s'all. If it weren't for you, I wouldn't be standing here talking to you now."

"Thanks, Duke. I'm just... Well, losing half my fireteam in one mission doesn't exactly make me feel qualified to lead, you know?"

"Sure, I get that. But you went into the heart of that nest and you made it out alive. That you're still standing when so many others aren't... *that's* why you're the right choice."

Duke gestured for them to continue down the corridor.

"Anyways, don't get too big a head. You're a lieutenant, not the grand bloody admiral. You're still a worthless grunt like the rest of us."

Ginger laughed and shook her head.

"Good to know you can still talk to me like I'm just a private, *Sergeant Sampson*."

Duke slapped her on the back as they approached the hangar doors.

"Some things never change, Ginger. Huh. *Sergeant*. Fits me pretty good, right?"

"Like a well-worn boot. You've earned it."

"We both have. Don't you go forgetting that."

They entered the hangar. Ginger felt her chest turn hollow. Just shy of three dozen marines stood at ease nearby, chatting amongst themselves as they waited for her to arrive. Nine fireteams in total. They straightened up and saluted the moment they saw her coming.

"Never gonna get used to that," Ginger muttered to herself.

Duke fell in line with the rest of Fireteam Sigma, which now consisted of three new, pimply faces Ginger probably should have memorised the names of. She felt ridiculous returning the salute. Duke shot her a conspiratorial wink.

Major Liu marched over from a neighbouring gunship. Ginger suddenly found herself saluting again. Then the major stuck out her hand.

"Congratulations, Lieutenant," she said as Ginger shook it. "You've got a good platoon there. Make sure they're ready for what's coming. We ship out in twenty."

"Yes, ma'am."

The major continued on and Ginger turned back to the expectant faces in front of her. She'd written out a big speech about how important the next operation was to humanity's ongoing survival, why the road ahead would be tougher than ever. But now she was away from the scribbles in her notepad, she couldn't remember a damn word of it.

Still. She had to say *something*.

"Right, I'll try and keep this short." Ginger nodded curtly. "We've got us some bugs to kill."

The WAR FOR NEW TERRA series will continue!

If you'd like to be alerted when the next book in the *War for New Terra* series is released, sign up for T.W.M. Ashford's mailing list at the website below.

www.twmashford.com

WANT AN EXCLUSIVE FINAL DAWN STORY?

Building a relationship with my readers is one of the best things about writing. Every now and then I send out newsletters with details on new releases, special offers and other bits of news relating to my books.

And if you sign up to the mailing list I'll even send you a **FREE** copy of *Before the Dawn*, an exclusive prequel story set immediately before *The Final Dawn*, the series set before *War for New Terra*.

Not bad, eh?

Sign up today at www.twmashford.com.

Enjoy this book? You can make a big difference.

Reviews are the most powerful tool in my arsenal when it comes to getting attention for my books. As an indie author, I don't have quite the same financial muscle as a New York publisher. But what I *do* have is something even more effective:

A committed and loyal bunch of readers.

Honest reviews of my books help bring them to the attention of other readers.

If you've enjoyed this book I would be very grateful if you could spend just five minutes leaving a review (it can be as short as you like) on the book's Amazon page.

Thank you very much.

ABOUT THE AUTHOR

T.W.M. Ashford is a British novelist living in London. You can call him Tom.

He's written hundreds of scripts and copy for some of the biggest companies in the world, and provides a variety of creative content for Mark Dawson's Self Publishing Formula. He's even been known to play a bass guitar on occasion.

But, of course, his main passion is writing fiction. He's currently setting up an interconnected space opera universe called the *Dark Star Panorama*, of which *Final Dawn* is the first series.

Send him an email at tom@twmashford.com. He'll enjoy the attention.

facebook.com/TWMAshford
instagram.com/ashfordtom

BOOKS BY T.W.M. ASHFORD

Books in the Dark Star Panorama Universe

Final Dawn Series

- The Final Dawn
- Thief of Stars
- A Dark Horizon
- The New World
- The Tin Soldiers
- Ghost of the Father

War for New Terra Series

- Sigma
- Iron Nest

Printed in Great Britain
by Amazon